THIN AIR, FAT CHANCE!

Joe buttoned up his jacket, pulled on the leather gloves, and tightened the chin strap on his helmet. He could feel the pulse in his temple beating like the bass drum in a heavy-metal band.

Grabbing the nearest steel upright with his left hand, he swung one leg up and straddled the padded edge of the basket. Trying to keep his eyes on the horizon, he pulled the other leg over.

Now Joe was perched on the edge of the basket. His feet dangled over the side. It was like sitting on a narrow tree limb.

For a moment, he forgot and glanced down. Instantly, his forehead broke into a cold sweat.

There was nothing between him and the ground but a few wispy clouds and half a mile of air. . . .

Books in THE HARDY BOYS CASEFILES™ Series

#1 DEAD ON TARGET
#2 EVIL, INC.
#3 CULT OF CRIME
#4 THE LAZARUS PLOT
#5 EDGE OF DESTRUCTION
#6 THE CROWNING TERROR
#7 DEATHGAME
#8 SEE NO EVIL
#9 THE GENIUS THIEVES
#12 PERFECT GETAWAY
#13 THE BORGIA DAGGER
#14 TOO MANY TRAITORS
#24 SCENE OF THE CRIME
#29 THICK AS THIEVES
#30 THE DEADLIEST DARE
#32 BLOOD MONEY
#33 COLLISION COURSE
#35 THE DEAD SEASON
#37 DANGER ZONE
#41 HIGHWAY ROBBERY
#42 THE LAST LAUGH
#44 CASTLE FEAR
#45 IN SELF-DEFENSE
#46 FOUL PLAY
#47 FLIGHT INTO DANGER
#48 ROCK 'N' REVENGE
#49 DIRTY DEEDS
#50 POWER PLAY
#52 UNCIVIL WAR
#53 WEB OF HORROR
#54 DEEP TROUBLE
#55 BEYOND THE LAW
#56 HEIGHT OF DANGER
#57 TERROR ON TRACK
#58 SPIKED!
#59 OPEN SEASON
#60 DEADFALL
#61 GRAVE DANGER
#62 FINAL GAMBIT
#63 COLD SWEAT
#64 ENDANGERED SPECIES
#65 NO MERCY
#66 THE PHOENIX EQUATION
#67 LETHAL CARGO
#68 ROUGH RIDING
#69 MAYHEM IN MOTION
#70 RIGGED FOR REVENGE
#71 REAL HORROR
#72 SCREAMERS
#73 BAD RAP
#74 ROAD PIRATES
#75 NO WAY OUT
#76 TAGGED FOR TERROR
#77 SURVIVAL RUN
#78 THE PACIFIC CONSPIRACY
#79 DANGER UNLIMITED
#80 DEAD OF NIGHT
#81 SHEER TERROR
#82 POISONED PARADISE
#83 TOXIC REVENGE
#84 FALSE ALARM
#85 WINNER TAKE ALL
#86 VIRTUAL VILLAINY
#87 DEAD MAN IN DEADWOOD
#88 INFERNO OF FEAR
#89 DARKNESS FALLS
#90 DEADLY ENGAGEMENT
#91 HOT WHEELS
#92 SABOTAGE AT SEA
#93 MISSION: MAYHEM
#94 A TASTE FOR TERROR
#95 ILLEGAL PROCEDURE
#96 AGAINST ALL ODDS
#97 PURE EVIL
#98 MURDER BY MAGIC
#99 FRAME-UP
#100 TRUE THRILLER
#101 PEAK OF DANGER
#102 WRONG SIDE OF THE LAW
#103 CAMPAIGN OF CRIME
#104 WILD WHEELS
#105 LAW OF THE JUNGLE
#106 SHOCK JOCK
#107 FAST BREAK
#108 BLOWN AWAY
#109 MOMENT OF TRUTH
#110 BAD CHEMISTRY
#111 COMPETITIVE EDGE
#112 CLIFF-HANGER
#113 SKY HIGH

Available from ARCHWAY Paperbacks

CASEFILES™

NO. 113

SKY HIGH

FRANKLIN W. DIXON

AN ARCHWAY PAPERBACK
Published by POCKET BOOKS
New York London Toronto Sydney Tokyo Singapore

This book is a work of fiction. Names, characters, places and incidents are products of the author's imagination or are used fictitiously. Any resemblance to actual events or locales or persons, living or dead, is entirely coincidental.

AN ARCHWAY PAPERBACK *Original*

An Archway Paperback published by
POCKET BOOKS, a division of Simon & Schuster Inc.
1230 Avenue of the Americas, New York, NY 10020

ISBN: 0-671-50454-1

First Archway Paperback printing July 1996

10 9 8 7 6 5 4 3 2 1

Printed in the U.S.A.

IL 6+

Chapter 1

"LOOK OUT, JOE!" Frank Hardy shouted. "You're going to hit him!"

There had been a big bang followed by the green pickup truck in front of them swerving wildly. Joe, Frank's younger brother by a year, spun the wheel, hit the brakes, and expertly sent their black van into a controlled skid.

In front of them the pickup truck rattled and shimmied. Frank saw several pieces of black tire fly out from the front passenger side as the truck continued to buck like a rodeo bull.

It took all of Joe's considerable driving skills to avoid slamming into the pickup's tailgate. He missed it by less than a foot. Traveling at fifty miles per hour along a country road, Joe knew that kind of collision could have done serious damage—and not just to the vehicles.

As they came to a stop nearly two hundred feet down the road, Frank turned back to see the pickup bouncing off into the ditch.

"Looks like he had a nasty blowout," said Chet Morton, who was riding in the backseat of the van. The truck had slammed halfway into the ditch, its tailgate sticking out onto the road and what was left of its front right tire half buried in mud.

They were about an hour's drive west of Bayport, their hometown, headed for a three-day ballooning meet at the century-old Wilderland Resort Hotel. They were really looking forward to the event, which had been widely publicized the past few days.

Chet was particularly excited because he had won a couple of free tickets for a balloon ride. He had found the winning ticket in a six-pack of Lift, a new soft drink, which was sponsoring the meet. It was good for two people, so he had invited his best friends, Frank and Joe. He figured since the first two tickets were free, he could buy a third one.

A girl in black shorts and a red-and-black shirt with a white collar climbed out of the pickup truck. She circled around to the passenger side to check out the tire.

Chet hopped out of the van and yelled to her, "Are you okay?"

She gave him a thumbs-up and yelled back, "Sure, thanks, but my truck's stuck."

After a moment's pause to look Chet over, she started toward the van. When she got there, she stuck out her hand for Chet to shake and said, "Hi, I'm Alicia Davidson."

Joe could see she was about seventeen, with short brown hair and a button nose. Pretty cute, he decided.

"Hop in," Joe said. "Are you headed to the balloon meet?"

"I'm in it," she said. "I was chasing my dad when my tire blew. Sorry, guys. I didn't mean to scare you."

"Scare *us?*" Chet said with a chuckle.

"What do you mean, chasing your dad?" Frank asked.

"He's right there," she said, pointing into the sky at about a seventy-five degree angle. The Hardys and Chet looked up and saw the brightly colored balloon floating about fifteen hundred feet above them.

"*Chasing* means I'm his support vehicle," Alicia said. "I try to stay in radio contact and meet him wherever he lands so we can break down the balloon and drive it back to the meet site. I guess I ought to give him a call to let him know what happened. Then, if you guys don't mind, I will hitch that ride. I can get somebody back at the meet to chase Dad. We'll worry about pulling the truck out later."

Alicia went over to her truck and was back in less than five minutes. She got in the back of the van with Chet. As they took off, Chet leaned over to look out the window.

"Hey," Chet said. "Isn't he awfully high? I thought these balloons just sort of floated above the trees."

"They do," Alicia said. "A couple of thousand feet above them."

"Oh," Chet said. "I knew that." He grinned at her and checked his watch.

"Don't worry about the time," Alicia said. "I know exactly where to go, and I'll make sure you meet all the right people as soon as we get there."

The van rounded a curve, and they saw the turnoff for the Wilderland Resort just ahead. As soon as they made the turn, they ran up against a slow-moving line of cars. Alicia flashed her balloonist's pass, and a guy wearing a bright orange vest over his T-shirt waved them past the line and on toward the main entrance of the resort.

They drove up the sloping driveway and reached the crest, where they were greeted by an impressive sight. On the wide meadow between them and the rustic main lodge stretched four long lines of brightly colored hot-air balloons bobbing in the breeze. The launching area was ringed by a white picket fence, and over the main gate was a big banner that read, "LIFT and the International Ballooning Club Welcome You to the International Balloonfest."

They parked near the fence and followed Alicia to a side gate, where she flashed her credentials again.

"I had no idea they'd be so huge," Chet said as they walked down an aisle made by two rows of balloons. Most of them were the usual inverted pear shapes, but not all. There was one that looked like an old-fashioned top hat. One of the biggest was in the shape of a gigantic bottle of Lift soda.

"Uh-oh," Chet said.

"What's wrong?" Frank asked.

Chet pointed to a sign that read, "Give yourself a LIFT. Hot-air balloon rides, $150 per person."

Chet's expression was gloomy. "I promised I'd give you guys a ride, and I invited both of you."

"Well, we're disinviting one of us," Frank said, pulling a quarter from his pocket. "Joe?"

"Heads," Joe said promptly.

Frank flipped the quarter, caught it, and

glanced down. "Heads it is," he said. "Okay, Chet. Joe and you get the ride."

"Chet, let me see that slip," Alicia said. Chet handed her his winning certificate. "It says you're to report to the hospitality tent for your assignment," she said. "I'll run over there and get it. I'll get someone to pick up my dad, too. Be right back."

She trotted over to the tent, went inside, and was back within three minutes holding another piece of paper.

"You guys will be riding in separate balloons for the Hare and Hounds," Alicia said. "Joe is going to fly with Paco Amaya, and Chet's with Dutch Festinger. They're both top pilots. It should be really exciting."

"What's the Hare and Hounds?" Chet asked.

"The first balloon is the Hare," Alicia answered. "He makes a flight and lands somewhere. The Hounds follow. Whoever lands closest to the Hare wins."

"That doesn't sound so hard," Joe said.

"You'd better believe it is," Alicia replied. "Remember, these balloons don't have engines or rudders. You go where the wind takes you. If it happens to change to the opposite direction after the Hare takes off, tough luck."

"I guess my brother has a few things to learn

about hot-air ballooning," Frank said, giving Joe a wink.

"This is the place to do it," Alicia said. "Come on, guys. Let's go meet Paco Amaya."

She took them over to a man in his thirties with long black hair pulled into a ponytail. He was wearing a checked Western shirt, jeans, and a tooled leather belt with a big turquoise and silver buckle. Alicia introduced them, then added, "Joe, Paco's going to take you up in the *Windrider.* He drove all the way here from New Mexico."

"Now, that's what I call commitment to your sport," Joe said.

"I'm going for the Lift Challenge," Amaya said. "That kind of prize doesn't come along very often."

"Not often enough for *you* to win one." A harsh voice cut in.

Frank looked around. A guy in a black jumpsuit was standing there, his gaze focused on Amaya. He had broad shoulders, a short thick neck, a square face, and blond crewcut. He reminded Frank of a character from a video game.

Amaya whirled around, took a step toward the man, and said, "Stay out of my business if you know what's good for you."

It looked as though the situation might get ugly, but it didn't because Alicia stepped in front of Amaya and said to the other guy, "Hi, Dutch. I was just coming to look for you. Dutch Festinger, meet Chet Morton, your passenger for the Hare and Hounds."

Festinger ignored Alicia to lock eyes with Amaya. "Good luck, Chet," Amaya said, meeting Festinger's gaze. "You never know what kind of ride you're going to get with this guy."

Festinger's face was turning red. Joe sized him up. He was at least three inches shorter than either Frank or himself. But he was powerfully built and obviously had a short fuse.

Festinger glanced from Frank to Joe and back again. Then he looked Chet up and down. He didn't seem very impressed.

"So," Festinger said, with a trace of a foreign accent. "Why don't you come with me? This is a waste of time. We'll go over the rules before we take off." Not waiting for Chet to reply, he turned and strode away.

Chet raised an eyebrow at Joe and Frank and said, "Here we go." Then he turned and hurried off to catch up with Festinger.

"Have a great ride," Alicia called after him.

"Let's go, Joe," Amaya said. "I'll show you the ropes."

Alicia watched them walk away. Then she turned to Frank. "Too bad we can't all just be friends," she said. "This is ballooning, after all—not some violent sport like boxing or wrestling."

"It doesn't matter what sport it is," Frank replied. "As long as there's a lot at stake, some people can't help holding grudges.

"What's the story with this guy Dutch?" Frank continued. "And where's he from?

"From Holland," Alicia replied.

"What's the problem between him and Amaya?" Frank said.

"Just competition," she said. "They're both going for the Aeronaut of the Year title. How they do in this meet will probably decide it. And, of course, there's the Lift Challenge on Sunday. First prize is one hundred thousand dollars."

"That's a lot of money," Frank said.

"I know," Alicia said. "But it doesn't mean they can't be good sports about it."

As Joe and Amaya walked down the field, a loud horn sounded. From the end of the row, a balloon that looked like a huge red apple rose into the air and began to move southward.

"There goes the Hare," Amaya said. "The rest of us take off in ten minutes. That's *Windrider* up ahead, with the red, white, and green panels."

Joe studied the balloon. It was as tall as a five-story building, with what looked like a straw laundry basket at the bottom. There were two men inside the basket working on the balloon, while a third held a cable outside to hold the balloon down. Suddenly a tongue of orange flame six feet long shot up from a coil of steel tubing into the open mouth of the balloon.

"That's the propane burner," Amaya explained. "It heats up the air inside the balloon. Since hot air weighs less than cooler air, the balloon rises."

"Pretty simple," Joe said. "Until you have to start navigating, I bet." He walked over to the basket. It really was woven of straw, with steel rods along the four edges that arched up to support the burner and steel tubing overhead. Inside, two propane tanks were strapped into the corners. There was an instrument panel with a compass, an altimeter, a couple of thermometers, and a dial labeled Vertical Speed Indicator. There was also a two-way radio handset.

"Here, Joe, you'll need these for protection," Amaya said, handing Joe a jean jacket, leather gloves, and a motorcycle helmet. "The burner gets really hot, and sometimes the landing can be pretty rough. Now, listen carefully . . ."

Amaya spent the next few minutes briefing Joe on takeoff, level flight, and landing. Then they took their places in the basket. While the two helpers held the edges of the basket, Amaya triggered another spurt of flame. The basket swayed slightly. It took Joe a moment to realize that they were already airborne—floating an inch or two above the ground.

Joe was trying to get used to the idea that he had left the ground when the horn sounded again. From every direction came the hissing roar of propane burners. Three balloons were already past treetop level, and the others were rising quickly in their wake.

Joe watched, fascinated by the spectacle. Then he happened to glance down. He caught his breath. They were already at least two hundred feet up with the ground receding fast.

The strangest part was that there was no real sense of motion: no noise, no vibration, no wind in the face. It was as if he, Amaya, and the enormous cloth globe above them were floating silently in one place while the entire earth scrolled past beneath them.

By now their view stretched for miles in all directions. Joe could see so much more from this basket than from the cockpit of an airplane. He relaxed and was trying to pick out some landmarks when a loud buzz broke his concentration.

"Will you take that?" Amaya asked, passing him the radio handset.

Joe identified himself. The voice in his ear said, "Balloon Five Seven Niner, this is Balloon One Zero One Echo, Dutch Festinger in command. I'm a hundred yards east of your position. I have an urgent condition. My deflation panel will not release. Request a visual assessment. Over."

"Hold on," Joe said. He quickly repeated the message to Amaya, who looked down and shook his head.

"What is it?" Joe asked.

"The deflation panel lets out the hot air," Amaya said. "If it's stuck, they can't land the balloon right. There's enough wind today to drag them all over the county. It'll probably tear that basket to shreds and them with it."

Chapter 2

JOE TRIED TO IMAGINE what would happen to Chet and Dutch Festinger if their basket was dragged across the ground at twenty or thirty miles an hour. It wouldn't be a pretty sight.

Joe stared across the distance that separated him from Festinger's blue- and green-striped balloon. It was about fifty yards away now, and they were flying at a slightly lower altitude. The curve of the balloon's bag hid the basket from him. He wondered if Chet realized he was in danger. What a way to end your first balloon ride.

"We've got to help them," Joe said.

"Nothing we can do," Amaya replied.

"Forget about your grudge with Dutch," Joe

said. "We can't just sit here and watch them crash."

"It has nothing to do with any grudge," Amaya said. "There just isn't anything we can do. They'll have to take their chances and hope for the best."

Joe thought for a few moments. "What did Dutch mean about a visual assessment? He's too far away for you to see much, isn't he?"

Amaya shrugged his shoulders. "I'd have to maneuver right next to them," he said. "Close enough to spot the problem."

"Maneuver?" Joe repeated. "How can you maneuver this thing? Alicia said they just go wherever the wind blows."

"That shows how little you know about it," Amaya snapped. "Maybe you can't steer it like a car or an airplane. But if you know what you're doing, you don't just follow the wind, you *use* it. If Dutch wants a visual assessment, I'll take *Windrider* right up to his craft and give him one."

Joe had an idea. "How strong are these balloons? I mean, is the fabric strong enough to hold somebody up?"

Amaya laughed. "You'd better hope so, amigo," he said. "Because that's all that's holding you up right this minute."

"Here's what I was thinking, Paco," Joe said. "If you can bring us close enough to see the problem, we'll also be close enough for me to jump down onto Dutch's balloon. Then I can just unsnag that deflation panel by hand."

"Man, are you loco?" Amaya exclaimed, staring at him. "We're over two thousand feet up."

"It's not that crazy," Joe said quickly. "I've got plenty of experience—skydiving, bungee jumping, rock climbing. Do you have any rope?"

Amaya paused for a second. He looked as if he might be coming around to the plan. "Maybe we could tie a drop line under your arms in case you slipped," Amaya said. "It's tested for a thousand pounds. Do you really think you can do this?"

"I know I can," Joe said.

"All right, let's try it," Amaya said, nodding at the radio handset. "Tell him to stay on course and we'll be there in a few minutes."

Joe picked up the handset again and sent Festinger a quick message. Meanwhile Amaya reached for the cord that controlled the burner. "I'm going to take us up a couple hundred feet," he said. "I'm pretty sure I can find a current up there that'll put us on a collision course with Festinger."

Joe swallowed. "A couple hundred feet?"

Amaya grinned at him. "Let me handle this part, Joe." He gave the balloon a quick blast of hot air with the burner, then watched carefully and waited. He explained to Joe that the key to maneuvering was the fact that there were different wind currents at different altitudes. All sorts of variables—ground contours, barometric pressure, altitude, and cloud cover—affected the wind direction. Controlling the balloon's flight path was simply a matter of judging the different wind directions quickly and accurately while changing altitude and making the correct adjustments. The burner heated the air to allow the balloon to ascend, and the deflation panel let the hot air out so the balloon could descend.

Amaya watched the other balloon with narrowed eyes, then said, "We'll be on top of them in a few minutes. You'd better get ready."

Joe buttoned up his jacket, pulled on the leather gloves, and tightened the chin strap on his helmet. Then he took the end of the webbing cord from Amaya and tied a bow line just under his arms, not too tight.

"I'll give you plenty of slack," Amaya said. "As soon as you're on the balloon, untie the line. Then I can put some distance between me and them. Got it?"

Joe nodded. Grabbing the nearest steel upright with his left hand, he swung one leg up and straddled the padded edge of the basket.

He could feel the vein in his temple beating like the bass drum in a heavy-metal band. Trying to keep his eyes on the horizon, he pulled the other leg over.

Now Joe was perched on the edge of the basket. His feet dangled over the side. It was like sitting on a narrow tree limb—half a mile up. He glanced down. There was nothing between him and the ground but a few wispy clouds.

He closed his eyes and concentrated on his breathing. He told himself that this was no different from psyching himself for a wrestling match. But he knew it was.

The top of Festinger's balloon was almost directly below them now, but they were still at least a hundred feet higher.

He felt Amaya's hand on his shoulder. "I'm taking us down slowly now," the balloonist told him. "Wait for my signal."

The blue and green stripes of Festinger's balloon seemed to swell slowly until they filled Joe's field of vision and blocked out the ground. He could clearly make out the big circular panel of the deflation vent and the web of cords that held it in place. The top surface of the other balloon was less than a dozen feet below now.

"Ready. Go!" Amaya said, tapping Joe's shoulder.

Joe took a deep breath and launched himself off the edge of the basket. As he fell, he wondered if this was what a squirrel felt like jumping from branch to branch of a tree. Before he knew it, his feet hit the surface of the other balloon. It was like landing on a gigantic inflated pillow. He flung himself forward, spreading his arms and legs wide. The fingers of his right hand found one of the nylon cords and closed tightly on it.

Pretty soon he realized there was little danger of falling off. His weight had made a dimple in the top of the balloon, so he was lying in the bottom of a little circular valley.

Joe quickly undid the knot in the webbing strap and slipped it from around his chest. Then he turned his head. There was *Windrider,* just above and to the left. He gave a thumbs-up signal. Amaya waved back, then started to reel in the drop line. Still gripping the cord, Joe raised himself on his elbows and took a look at the deflation panel.

He spotted the problem right away. The cord that operated the panel passed through a metal ring at the center of the panel. But just before it reached the ring, the cord was wrapped around a yellow plastic tent stake. There was no way it could work properly. Joe inched his way over, untangled the stake, and gave the cord a yank. It slid free, opening up the deflation panel. He turned and gave Amaya the thumbs-up again. Before starting to creep over to the edge of the panel, he carefully tucked the tent stake inside his jacket pocket.

As Joe reached the edge of the panel, he felt the fabric starting to move under him. He quickly grabbed a support cable in each hand. There was a sudden burst of warm air from the open vent. He peeked down through the opening. It was pretty weird. He was looking straight down through the balloon at the basket some fifty feet below him. He could even make out the tops of Chet's and Festinger's helmets.

Then he felt the balloon start to swing sideways, and he realized that the basket must have touched ground. Quickly, he gathered his legs under him. He waited until he saw grass beneath him, a dozen feet down, then pushed off. Like a parachutist, he landed with his legs bent and did a quick tuck-and-roll. A moment later, everything went blue and green as the feather-light fabric of the balloon bag draped itself over him.

Joe began to crawl toward what he hoped was the edge of the balloon. Then, abruptly, someone was pulling the material off him.

It was Chet. "Joe, are you all right?" he asked.

Joe took a deep breath and got to his feet. "I'm fine," he said, brushing himself off. "How about you?"

"Okay," Chet said. "But I can't believe you just did that. Of all the daredevil stunts I've ever seen you do, this one has to—"

"Wait a second," Joe interrupted. "You should be thanking me. You guys could have wiped out."

"He's right," Festinger said. He stepped forward, shook Joe's hand, and said, "We owe you thanks, Joe. That was very courageous. Now I would like to know why the deflation cord did not work."

Joe was about to tell him about the tent stake when he saw a blue four-wheel-drive utility wagon bumping across the pasture toward them. Even before it came to a full stop, the rear door flew open. Frank jumped out and jogged over.

"Nice work, Joe," Frank said. "That was a pretty impressive stunt."

Joe grinned at his brother. "How'd you find out? The radio?"

"No, I was watching with binoculars the whole time," Frank replied.

Joe looked past Frank. Two men and a woman had gotten out of the car and were coming toward them. The man in the lead was mostly bald, with only a fringe of white hair and a closely trimmed white beard. His expression was grim. Just behind the man was a dark-haired young woman in black jeans and a black sleeveless turtleneck. A worried-looking middle-aged man in khakis and a blue blazer brought up the rear.

"Who are your friends?" Joe murmured to Frank.

"The guy with the beard is Fred Elwell," Frank said, "president of the International Ballooning Club. The woman's Marie Thibault, his executive assistant. The guy in the blazer is Arneson. He's a big shot with the company that makes Lift soda."

The three came over and introduced themselves to Joe. Elwell shook Joe's hand, then said, "Excuse us, fellows, but we need to ask Dutch a few questions."

A big shadow blocked the sun for a moment. Joe looked back over his shoulder and saw that it was Amaya's balloon setting down on the grass about fifty yards away. When he turned back, Elwell and the others were clustered around Festinger.

"I have no idea why it jammed," Joe heard Festinger say. "I did a full preflight checkup. Everything was in perfect order."

Joe joined the group. He reached inside his jacket and pulled out the tent stake. "I found this tangled in the deflation panel cord," he said. "The cord was wrapped around it twice. There was no way that panel could open."

Everyone took a long look at the yellow stake in Joe's hand. "Where could it have come from?" Elwell said.

"I keep some in my equipment box, for staking out the balloon envelope when it gets breezy," Festinger answered. "I will go check."

Festinger stepped over to the basket of his balloon and rummaged around inside. When he returned, he had a matching yellow stake in one hand and a mallet in the other. "I have six stakes," he announced. "There are only five in there now. This is very serious. Someone took one of these and stopped up my deflation panel with it. This was no accident. I *demand* an official investigation." He was beginning to sound angry.

At that point Amaya came jogging across the field toward them. "Everybody okay?" he called out.

"Just fine," Joe said.

"Any idea how the cord got jammed?" Amaya asked, a little out of breath as he joined the group.

"Well . . ." Joe said.

Before he could finish, Festinger faced Amaya. He spoke in an aggressive tone. "Maybe we should be asking that question of someone like you. Someone who would benefit directly from knocking me out of the Hare and Hounds."

"In case you didn't notice, I dropped out of the competition to save your sorry rig from ripping itself to shreds," Amaya said. "So maybe you should thank me instead of accusing me. And maybe you should try to figure out how to take better care of your equipment."

"Watch how you speak to me, young man!" Festinger shouted, pointing the stake in his left hand directly at Amaya's face. "If there's another incident like this, you'll be sorry."

"Are you threatening me?" Amaya said, stepping up to Festinger and grabbing a fistful of his jacket lapel in his right hand. "Because if you are, it's a very stupid move." Amaya punctuated each of the last two words with two hard shakes of Festinger's lapel.

"That's enough out of you!" Festinger yelled, his face red with fury. He hesitated a fraction of a second, then, in a lightning-quick move, he grabbed both of Amaya's arms with powerful hands, sidestepped him, and threw him to the ground. Before Amaya had a chance to push himself to his feet, Festinger jumped on top of him and raised the mallet, ready to smash it down on top of Amaya's head.

Chapter 3

As Amaya raised his arms to shield his face, Fred Elwell shouted, "Stop it, Dutch!" But Festinger gave no sign that he had heard. As he started the mallet on its downward swing, Frank lunged forward to grab his wrist. He was a fraction of a second late, but it was enough to slow down the murderous blow. It was also enough for Amaya to draw his knees up to his chest and kick hard with both feet.

Amaya's blow caught Festinger in his stomach. Festinger let out a grunt, dropped the mallet, and staggered backward, clutching his midsection. Joe and Chet each grabbed him by an arm and held on tight.

Amaya bounced to his feet and started

toward his opponent, fists clenched. But Frank quickly stepped in front of him while Joe and Chet yanked Festinger out of reach.

"Take it easy, Paco," Frank said. "The fight's over."

"That pig tried to kill me," Amaya said, dodging around Frank and pulling a switch-blade out of his back pocket. He flicked it open. "I ought to cripple him for life."

Before Amaya could pounce on Festinger, Frank had grabbed his wrist. "That's enough," Frank said. Amaya tried to pull loose, but Frank tightened his grip and pulled harder. "Put the knife away, now," he said.

Amaya went slack and said, "Okay, okay." Frank let go of his wrist, and Amaya put away his knife.

"What's the matter with this guy?" Amaya asked, glaring past Frank at Festinger. "When's he going to learn to stop picking fights?"

"When you learn to stop tampering with other people's equipment," Festinger snarled, trying to shake loose from Chet and Joe.

"This guy is completely loco," Amaya said. "Why would I sabotage his balloon, then go rescue him and miss my chance to win the Hare and Hounds? Dutch, if it wasn't for Joe and me, you'd still be floating at two thousand feet, sweating like a pig and wondering what to do next."

"Pigs don't sweat," Chet said. "It's a scientific fact."

Chet's remark had everybody speechless for a few moments. Joe appreciated his effort at humor. It made him want to laugh out loud, but he knew it wasn't enough to take the edge off the tempers of the two rival balloonists.

"All right, can we get a few facts straight?" Frank asked, focusing first on Amaya, then on Festinger. "Dutch, you checked your balloon before you inflated it, right?"

"I already said so," Dutch muttered. "There was nothing wrong with the deflation panel."

"And once the balloon was inflated," Frank continued, "there was no way anyone could have reached the spot where Joe found that tent stake, right? So the stake must have been put there between the time you did your preflight check and the time the balloon was inflated."

"That's right," Joe said. He looked over at Festinger. "How long do you think that was?"

"How would I know?" Festinger replied sullenly. "Five minutes, ten minutes. But to twist the stake into the cord, how long would *that* take? A few seconds."

Frank turned to Amaya. "Where were you

when Dutch's balloon was being inflated?" he asked.

Amaya shrugged. "I have no idea," he replied. "I was all over the place. I have a lot of friends in this business. I was saying hello to them."

"This isn't getting us anywhere," the man in the blazer, Arneson, declared. "Fred, we'd better get back to the hotel. We've got to meet some reporters in twenty minutes, and they're going to be asking about what happened. We need to go over our approach."

Amaya gave him a curious look. "Excuse me, I don't think we've met," he said. "I'm Paco Amaya."

"This is Max Arneson, Paco," Elwell said. "He's here on behalf of our sponsor, Lift. Of course, he already knows who you guys are."

"You mean you're the guy with the hundred grand?" Amaya asked, smiling. "That's the kind of man I like to meet."

"Of course you would—in a dark alley," Festinger said.

Amaya's jaw muscles tightened, but all he did was glare wordlessly at the Dutchman.

A blue pickup truck appeared at the edge of the meadow, followed closely by a gray van. The two vehicles stopped near the 4x4, and their passengers got out.

"Excuse me, people," Amaya said. "My

ground crew's here, and we've got some work to do." He went over to meet the group from the gray van. Without saying a word, Festinger walked over to the other group.

Frank, Joe, and Chet huddled briefly. "Listen," Frank said in a low voice. "I'm going to get a ride back with Elwell. We can meet back at the hospitality tent, okay? Joe, why don't you stick with Paco? And, Chet, you do the same with Dutch. Keep your ears open. Maybe we can figure out who's doing what to whom."

Joe volunteered to help Paco Amaya and his crew fold up *Windrider* while Chet managed to persuade Dutch Festinger and his crew to let him tag along with them.

As the rest of the group walked back toward the official 4x4 wagon, Frank fell into step with Marie Thibault.

"Everything okay?" Frank asked her. They had chatted amicably earlier in the day, but ever since Dutch Festinger's "accident" and Joe's rescue, she'd been quiet.

"Oh, fine," she said. "I've just got a lot on my mind—all the stuff I have to get done for the meet—and then these guys start a fight in front of our main sponsor."

Frank noticed that she had tiny silver balloons dangling from each ear. "I like your earrings," he said.

"Thanks," she replied. "I figure they're

about as close as I'll ever come to having my own balloon," she added with a laugh.

"Would you want to?" Frank asked. "It seems like an awfully expensive sport."

"Brilliant deduction," Marie Thibault said. "Buying the balloon is just the beginning. If you really want to see big bills, check out what it takes to keep a balloon up and running. I guess I'm lucky. Working with Fred, I get to go to a lot of events, meet everybody, take a few rides in my spare time. Just last month we went to a meet in England."

"Sounds great," Frank said as he climbed into the backseat of the 4x4 after her.

From the front passenger seat, Arneson said, "I'm glad to know something sounds great. Because so far, today has been one big disaster."

Fred Elwell settled behind the wheel and started the engine. "Come now, Max," he said as he pulled onto the road. "Things go wrong at any meet. So we had one near-accident. That's not so bad."

"Accident?" Arneson said. "I think it's pretty obvious it wasn't an accident. And we'd better find out who did it pretty quickly and *very* quietly. I stuck my neck way out to get Lift to sponsor this competition. We have a big investment in this thing. I still think the fit is terrific, but it's the first time. If things don't work out exactly right, there won't be a next time."

"I can see that," Elwell said, shaking his head. "I suppose we'll have to mount an investigation. How about your corporate security department? Maybe they—"

"Sorry," Arneson said quickly. "They're basically just plant guards. What about that company you hired for the meet?"

Elwell shook his head again. "They're fine for directing traffic and crowd control, but I wouldn't trust them with a delicate matter like this."

Frank saw his opening. Leaning forward, he said, "Maybe my brother and I can help. We've had a lot of experience as detectives, and we can definitely keep any investigation discreet."

"I appreciate the offer," Elwell began, "but we shouldn't be discussing this in front of you. If your brother hadn't pulled off that stunt with Dutch Festinger's deflation panel . . ."

"Wait a minute, Fred," Arneson said. He turned around in his seat and focused on Frank. "What did you say your name was?"

"Hardy. Frank Hardy."

"You wouldn't be related to Fenton Hardy, would you?" Arneson asked.

"He's my dad," Frank replied.

Arneson smiled. "Excellent. Fred, that's our

answer. I don't know if you're acquainted with Fenton Hardy, but he's a top-notch private investigator. He's done several jobs for our corporation. If these kids have their dad's endorsement, then I'd go with them."

Elwell drummed his fingers on the steering wheel. After a few moments of silence, he said, "Frank, do you think you and Joe could manage to hang around and ask questions without attracting a lot of attention?"

"Sure," Frank said. "We already know Dutch and Paco. That gives us a head start. And why would anybody suspect something if we ask questions? We're curious about ballooning, that's all. We're just a couple of teenagers who fell in love with the sport, right?"

"Right," Elwell said with a decisive nod. "When we get back to the Wilderland, I'll make out guest passes for you, your brother, and your friend. That way, you'll be able to go anywhere you need to. You fellows should be at the welcoming banquet tonight at the hotel. If there's anything else I can do to help your investigation, just tell me. And remember, we need speed. But more than that, we need discretion."

The International Ballooning Club had set up a temporary office just inside the main entrance of the hotel building. The oak desks and glass-fronted bookcases in the office probably hadn't been moved since World War I. The big iron safe in the corner looked even older. The computer system and fax machine, however, were completely up to date. Marie Thibault entered information about Chet and the two Hardys, then printed out the three passes.

"Here you go," she said, handing them to Frank. "Good luck."

Frank was eager to tell Joe and Chet about their new official status. He hurried out of the hotel and across the front lawn to the hospitality tent. As he neared the tent, he saw Alicia Davidson coming from the other direction. She was walking with a tall, gangly man in his late twenties. His sandy hair, partly hidden by a New York Yankees cap, just brushed the collar of his scuffed brown leather jacket. He looked like someone who might have played right field for his college baseball team.

"Frank," Alicia said. "I just heard what Joe did. That's amazing. Oh—this is Mark Svoboda. He just won the Hare and Hounds event."

"Congratulations," Frank said.

Svoboda nodded curtly at Frank and turned to Alicia. "I've got to check my messages back at the hotel," he said. "I'll be right back."

"You must be really proud of your brother," Alicia said. "So what was the problem?"

Frank explained about the jammed deflation panel. "You guys are right, Frank. There's no way that could have been an accident," she said. "There's something else you should know about."

"What is it?" Frank asked.

Alicia shook her head slowly. "Something that happened a couple of months ago at a balloon meet in Lubbock, Texas. A lot of the top competitors were at that one, too. There was a suspicious accident that kept Mark Svoboda, the guy you just met, from winning the main event."

"Oh? Did they find out who was responsible?" Frank asked.

"No," Alicia told him. "There wasn't even any real proof that it wasn't an accident. But there were plenty of rumors."

"About what?" Frank said.

"About Mark's main rival, the guy who won the grand prize at Lubbock and the points that went with it."

"Who was that?" Frank asked.

"You already met him," Alicia replied. "It was Paco Amaya."

Chapter 4

"PACO?" FRANK STARED at Alicia. "Do you really think he was responsible?"

"I don't know," Alicia replied. "Mark sure thought so. As far as I know, he still does."

"What exactly happened?" Frank asked.

Alicia was hesitant to continue. "It doesn't matter. I'm sorry I said anything. Just forget it, okay?"

"Sure, if you say so," Frank agreed. He made a mental note to check into it later. "So, what are the big events this weekend?"

"Tomorrow there's a novice race that I'm entered in. I've flown a lot with my dad, of course, but this'll be my first event totally on my own."

"You must be excited," Frank said.

"I can't wait." Her eyes gleamed. "Then, of course, the really big event is the Lift Challenge on Sunday. It's one of the biggest prizes in ballooning."

"Who are the favorites?" Frank asked.

"Well, the three you already met: Dutch Festinger, Mark Svoboda, and Paco Amaya," Alicia said. "They're all good at distance events."

Mark Svoboda rejoined them. Whatever his business had been, it hadn't done anything to cheer him up. He seemed to be as gloomy as ever.

"We were just talking about the Lift Challenge," Alicia told Svoboda.

Frank asked, "How does it work? Is it a race?"

"Not exactly," Svoboda replied as his expression became a little more animated. "Each contestant gets a propane tank with a premeasured amount of fuel. The one who manages to go the farthest on it wins. A lot depends on finding the right altitude, with a strong, steady wind."

"Hey, Frank," Joe yelled.

Frank looked around and saw Chet and Joe moving toward them.

"They don't look any worse for their adventure," Alicia said.

Chet, a few steps ahead of Joe, said, "Hi, Alicia."

"I hope you won't let what happened spoil ballooning for you, will you?" Alicia asked.

"Not a chance," Chet answered.

"Then you'll be happy to hear we're going to be here for the whole meet," Frank said. "Fred Elwell gave all three of us guest passes. He even invited us to the banquet this evening."

Alicia said, "Hey, that's great. You can sit with me and my dad, if you like."

"Thanks, that'll be fun," Frank replied.

Alicia introduced Chet and Joe to Svoboda and added, "Chet was Dutch's passenger in the Hare and Hounds today. Dutch must have been really upset by what happened."

"He was pretty worked up," Chet said. "He and Paco got into a tussle after they landed. Dutch won't let it go. All he could talk about on the way back was how he was going to get even with Paco."

"So he thinks Paco caused the accident?" Svoboda asked, his eyes narrowing.

"Well," said Chet, who realized he'd said too much, "let's just say Dutch was upset, that's all."

They all paused for a beat. Then Alicia glanced at her watch and said, "Oops, I'm running late. I'll see you guys later."

"What are you fellows doing between now and the banquet?" Svoboda asked as Alicia hurried away. "I've got some free time. I'd be glad to give you a tour and answer any questions."

What Frank really wanted at that point was a chance to question the people who'd been acting as Festinger's ground crew during inflation. Had one of them seen anyone—Paco Amaya, for instance—hanging around? He also needed to get Joe and Chet alone, so he could fill them in on his conversation with Fred Elwell and find out what they had learned from Festinger and Amaya on the drive back.

On the other hand, he wasn't going to pass up a chance to be shown around by one of the top competitors. Being seen with Mark Svoboda would give the three of them major credentials with the other participants in the meet. That was bound to help their investigation.

"Great," Frank said. "Where do we start?"

"Have you seen *Earthquest* yet?" Svoboda asked.

"Is that a movie?" Chet said.

Svoboda managed a small smile. "No, it's Harris Scott's Rozier-type helium balloon," he said. "It's one of the highlights of the meet. Harris designed and built it for an around-the-world flight."

"Around the world?" Joe exclaimed. "It must be enormous."

"Two hundred fifty feet high," Svoboda told him.

Frank looked out over the field. Some of the balloons were pretty big—the one shaped like a bottle of Lift, for instance—but there was nothing even approaching the size Svoboda was describing. "Where is it?" he asked.

"Right over there," Svoboda said. He pointed to a metal capsule no larger than the Hardys' van. Frank thought it looked like a tiny submarine. "It's pressurized for high-altitude flying and designed to survive a ditching in the ocean."

"Where's the rest of it?" Chet asked. "The balloon part?"

"And what's a 'rosier'?" Frank added.

"I'll let Harris explain everything," Svoboda said. "Come on, he loves to tell people about it."

Practically everything about Harris Scott was red—his hair, his beard, his face, and even his polo shirt. He was sitting in a folding deck chair next to *Earthquest.* He had a clipboard on his lap and a ballpoint pen between his teeth. He looked up as they approached and put the pen down to say hello. After introductions, Frank and Chet asked their questions.

"The balloon is back in New Mexico, where

I'm based," Scott replied. "This capsule should be good for years, but the balloon bag is so delicate that I get only one use out of it. It costs over a hundred thousand dollars to replace."

"How does it compare to the one Joe and Chet rode in today?" Frank asked.

"*Earthquest* is really two balloons, one inside the other," Scott explained. "The smaller one is always filled with helium, and the larger one can be inflated with hot air. That way, I don't have to constantly use fuel to stay aloft, the way an ordinary hot-air balloon does. The idea goes all the way back to Jean-François de Rozier, who made the first manned balloon flight in Paris, in 1783. That's why this is called a Rozier-type balloon."

"Mind if the guys look inside?" Svoboda asked.

"Go ahead and take a peek," Scott replied.

Frank followed Joe and Chet over to the little craft. He could see why Scott might not want them to go inside. The interior was small and cramped. There were two reclining pilot seats, facing panels of instruments and switches. It reminded Frank of an early space capsule that he'd seen on a visit to the Smithsonian.

"How long will you be in the air?" Joe asked.

Scott said, "I figure about ten to twelve days. Once we hit the jet stream, we should be going up to two hundred miles an hour. It'll be quite an adventure." He smiled and added, "But the toughest part is raising the money to pay for it."

"If I win the Lift Challenge on Sunday," Svoboda said, "I'm planning to contribute some of the prize to *Earthquest.* Harris, did you make your pitch to the Lift people?"

"I got the brush-off," Scott said, his voice tightening. "They don't like the odds against me, I guess. Maybe they heard about what happened to Rozier."

"What was that?" Chet asked.

"A couple of years after that first flight, he tried to fly across the English Channel," Scott said. "His balloon caught fire in midair. So he set a different kind of record. He was the first person ever to be killed in a balloon accident."

The banquet that evening was held in the dining room of the Wilderland Resort Hotel. It was a room the size of a basketball court. Its wooden ceiling was held up by thick logs that were dark with a patina of age. The tall windows at the far end of the room offered a spectacular view of the lake beside the hotel and the mountains surrounding it.

Joe finished his last bite of cherry pie à la

mode, sat back in his chair, and let out a contented sigh. He was stuffed. Across the table, Chet and Alicia were talking intently. Frank was chatting with Alicia's dad, Dave Davidson.

Joe glanced around the room. It seemed like a pretty happy group except for the two factions that were giving off vibrations against each other. Paco Amaya was at a table near the windows, surrounded by a group of his friends. Dutch Festinger was at the opposite end of the room, near the big stone fireplace. He, too, was surrounded by cronies.

Were the bitter rivals circling their wagons for another nasty confrontation before the weekend was over? Joe wondered, if he had to choose, which one of them he would trust. So far, he had to give the nod to Amaya since Festinger seemed to be an obvious aggressor. But Joe was starting to have his doubts about Amaya, too. Particularly after Frank had mentioned the rumors in connection with Mark Svoboda's "accident" at the Lubbock meet. And Festinger did have plenty of reason to be upset . . .

At the head table, just a few yards away, Fred Elwell stood up and tapped a spoon on his water glass. The buzz of conversation in the room gradually died away.

"Friends and fellow balloonists," he began, "on behalf of the International Ballooning

Club, I'd like to welcome you to this, our most important meet of the year. We're particularly proud that we're able to host the Lift Challenge, with its magnificent prize, and I'd like to ask you to give a really warm welcome to the person who made it possible—Max Arneson, vice-president of marketing for Lift. By now, I'm sure you're all familiar with their slogan, When you need a Lift . . . Their support has certainly given a huge lift to the sport we all love so much. Max, would you like to say a few words?"

As applause broke out, Arneson got to his feet and waved. "Thank you all," he said. "We're very proud to sponsor this event, and especially the Lift Challenge. Before I came here, I tried to think how to show you, as clearly as possible, just how committed we are to your fine organization and the wonderful sport of ballooning. I thought about bringing an enormous copy of the winner's check. But we've all seen that dozens of times on TV. So, instead . . ."

He gestured toward the entrance. TV lights came on as two uniformed men walked in, carrying a closed case of Lift between them. An armed guard followed them.

Frank turned to Joe and whispered, "Are they afraid somebody'll hijack their case of soft drinks?"

Before Joe could reply, the men reached the front of the room and set the soda case on the table in front of Arneson, then stepped to the side. Arneson opened the flaps of the carton and tipped it up to show the contents to the room. The carton was filled almost to the brim with banded packets of crisp new hundred-dollar bills.

"One hundred thousand dollars in fresh U.S. currency," Arneson said. "Every penny of which goes to the winner of this year's Lift Challenge."

As Arneson continued his speech, Joe noticed a waiter making his way to the head table and handing an envelope to Elwell. Obviously puzzled, Elwell opened the envelope and glanced inside. His expression changed from puzzlement to surprise and then to worry.

Elwell looked up, caught Joe's eye, and made a sideways gesture with his head. Then he stood up and walked toward the back of the room. Joe tapped Frank on the shoulder, and the two of them followed the IBC president out into the corridor.

"I wish I hadn't agreed to that stunt with the cash," Elwell said when they were alone. "I think we've got a big problem. Look at what I just got."

Joe unfolded the sheet of paper and held it

so that Frank could read it at the same time. The message was short and to the point:

> Festinger's "accident" was just the beginning. Unless you want more of the same, be ready to hand over $100,000. Otherwise, somebody dies.

Chapter 5

FRANK REREAD THE NOTE, then glanced up at Elwell. "Looks like this is more than just a sick joke," he said.

"It looks like a serious attempt at extortion," Elwell said.

"How do you want to handle it?" Joe asked.

"If it were up to me, I'd turn it over to the police," Elwell replied. "I don't believe in giving in to threats. And even if I did, the IBC doesn't have anything close to that kind of money."

"The note says 'hand over a hundred thousand dollars,' " Joe said. "I guess that means the Lift Challenge prize money."

Elwell pursed his lips and nodded. "I'm sure

whoever it is figures if Lift is willing to spend that much to get good publicity, they'd be willing to spend the same to avoid bad publicity," Elwell said. "And he may be right. The problem is, if we do go to Arneson and the Lift people and they do pay the money, then they'd probably never dream of getting involved in a ballooning event again."

"Arneson's not going to blame the IBC," Joe said. "It's not your fault some crook decided to get rich quick off your event."

"It's not really a question of fault," Elwell replied. "Any kind of bad association can really ruin a product's reputation. Back in the 1950s, lots of major car manufacturers had factory-sponsored racing teams. Every time a company won a big race, it helped to sell cars. Then one of the top cars crashed into the crowd during the big twenty-four hour race at Le Mans. Dozens of people were killed. It was an accident. Even though its cars were world champions, the car maker quit racing and didn't go back to it for more than twenty years. If we start having balloon accidents, Lift will be forced to pull out no matter whose fault it is."

"I see your point," Joe said. "So where does this leave us?"

"We've got to figure out a way to stop this

extortionist without blowing the lid off the whole thing," Frank said.

"I'd better get back inside before everybody wonders where I've gone," Elwell said. "Why don't you and your friend Chet meet me and Arneson in my office for a strategy session after the banquet? If you need a place to stay, I can arrange for it then, too."

"We were planning on going home to Bayport," Frank said.

"Then be sure to be back by dawn tomorrow, and plan on sticking around through Sunday, too," Elwell said.

"Right," Joe said, holding up the note. "We'd like to keep this for analysis for the time being."

Elwell hesitated. "All right," he said. "But I may need to show it to Arneson and the authorities—if it comes to that."

Elwell returned to the dining room as Frank and Joe moved closer to one of the old-fashioned wall lamps to study the extortion message.

Joe held the paper up to the light. "No watermark," he reported. "It's ordinary copier and printer paper. Could be from anywhere."

"That looks like fourteen-point Helvetica typeface," Frank added. "It comes on a lot of laser printers. Not much help there."

"Maybe not," Joe said. "But what about the

chain of events? Whoever wrote this knew about the incident with Dutch's balloon, and probably wrote it *after* that happened. And we know at least one place here with a laser printer—the IBC office."

"Let's check it out with Marie Thibault," Frank said. "She could probably tell us everyone who had access to the office."

There was a burst of applause from inside the dining room. It gradually died down until all they could hear was a loud murmur of conversation and a rustle of commotion as everyone got ready to leave. A few moments later the dining-room doors swung open and the crowd started to exit, at first as a trickle, then as a flood.

"Do you see Chet?" Frank asked Joe as they stood and scanned the faces.

"There he is," Joe replied. He was with Alicia Davidson and her dad.

Joe waved, and Chet edged through the crowd to join them. "What happened to you guys?" he asked. "One minute you were there. The next, I looked up and you were gone."

Joe told him about the extortion note. "We're supposed to meet with Elwell and Arneson in the IBC office now," Joe said. "We need to work up a plan."

"Okay, I'm with you," Chet said. "Alicia asked if we'd give her a hand inflating her balloon for the novice event in the morning. Do you think we can get here early?"

"Sure," Frank replied. "Elwell wants us here early, too. How does five-thirty sound?"

"Ouch," Chet said with a grin. "But I guess when duty calls, sleep has to wait. I'll go tell Alicia. Meet you at the office."

The office door was locked. Joe and Frank waited for Elwell and Arneson. They showed up within a few minutes, and Chet was close behind them. They all went into the office and sat down.

"I told Max about the note," Elwell began. "He agrees with me that we have to take it seriously, especially after what happened this afternoon."

Frank asked, "What do you mean by taking it seriously? Bringing in the police?"

"No cops," Arneson said quickly. "We've got crews from all the networks and two major sports programs coming here for the Lift Challenge, not to mention all the print reporters. If they find out about this extortion attempt, *that* will be the story—and forget about the Challenge."

"I'm sure we could persuade the cops to keep it quiet," Joe said.

Arneson gave a snort of disbelief. "Sure, we could ask," he said. "But what local cop would be able to resist getting his shot at ten minutes of nationwide fame? Look, guys, if you've changed your minds about working with us on this, fine. We understand. We'll hire a PI firm. But there's no way we're calling in the authorities at this point. I'd rather pay off the extortionist."

"You'd risk a hundred thousand dollars?" Chet asked.

"In untraceable bills?" Joe added.

"Look," Arneson responded. "We're already investing a lot more than that in this. We're paying a lot of the club's expenses, plus we launched a major publicity campaign for the meet. We think it's a good investment. The ballooning sponsorship is the focus of our whole ad campaign for Lift. People are going to think of Lift every time they see a balloon. Any kind of negative publicity at this point blows the whole thing. Better to spend the extra hundred grand to protect our investment."

"Right," Frank said, "but meanwhile, we have a chance to track down the crook. We've already got a couple of leads. Plus, this is just the first contact. Once we get the next demand, we can set up a trap. Meantime, we develop our leads."

"They have my endorsement, Max," Elwell said.

"Okay," Arneson said. "But you boys had

better step on it. We don't have much time. As soon as this guy spells out the payout arrangement, we're going to have to respond."

Joe hated it when anyone called them "boys." Usually, it was Bayport Police Chief Ezra Collig who did it, and Joe was convinced that was done strictly to annoy them. Okay, so Arneson doesn't know any better, Joe thought, but once we catch this slimeball, I doubt he'll be saying "you boys" anymore.

"Let's move out," Joe said to Frank and Chet. "We need to get an early start in the morning," he added with a smile and a wink in Chet's direction.

"Oh—before we leave, do you think we could have a quick word with Marie Thibault?" Frank asked.

"She's already turned in," Elwell replied. "She told me she was exhausted after the banquet and was going straight to bed. Can it wait until the morning?"

Frank shrugged. "I guess it'll have to." He gave a quick wave good night and trudged out to the parking field with Chet and Joe for the hour-long drive back to Bayport.

The next morning Joe, Frank, and Chet drove up the approach road to the Wilderland Resort just as the sky was starting to lighten. Joe parked near the gate and got out of the van to peer up at the unbroken layer of gray, low-hanging clouds. "Do balloons go up on a day like this?" he wondered aloud.

"They'd better," Chet said. "Otherwise, we got up in the middle of the night for nothing."

"There's no rain in the forecast," Frank pointed out. "Mild winds. Possibly some fog or haze. Let's see what Alicia thinks."

"Alicia said she's about halfway down the second row," Chet said. "It's a yellow balloon with red diamonds."

On the field, the balloons were at different stages of being inflated. Joe spotted Alicia in jeans and a brown leather jacket. She was fastening a series of steel cables to the balloon's basket, which was lying on its side.

"Good morning, gentlemen!" she called with a big smile. "You're just in time to help me lay out the envelope."

Under her direction, Chet and the Hardys began unrolling and stretching out the light, strong fabric. After Alicia double-checked the cables and control lines and set out a fire extinguisher, she asked Joe and Frank to hold open the mouth of the balloon. She and Chet wheeled over a fan powered by a lawnmower engine and got it started.

"We start by filling the balloon about halfway with cool air," she explained. "Then I'll use the burner to add warm air and finish inflating it."

As the air rushed into the balloon, Joe could feel it taking shape in his hands. Alicia climbed into the basket, which was still lying on its side, and aimed the propane burner at the opening between Joe and Frank. Joe took a backward step as the long, orange-blue flame lanced past him.

The balloon bag was stirring now, beginning to rise off the ground. The basket, linked to it by the cables, started to tilt toward an upright position. Alicia held on to the padded railing with one hand while continuing to operate the burner with the other.

Joe frowned as he noticed a small blue flame at the bottom of the burner, where the feeder pipe from the tank was attached. That wasn't supposed to be there, was it? He was going to say something to warn Alicia, but before he could, a stream of burning propane raced along the pipe to the support and into the basket.

At almost the same instant, a splash of the flaming liquid spilled onto the back of Alicia's leather jacket and set her ablaze.

Chapter 6

"ALICIA, WATCH OUT!" Joe shouted. "You're on fire!"

Startled, Alicia released the wire that controlled the burner valve. She turned to look over her shoulder and saw the flames spreading fast. She struggled desperately with the front of her jacket, trying to pull it off.

Joe looked around for the fire extinguisher. There it was, on the ground a few feet from the basket. He lunged for it. Out of the corner of his eye, he saw Frank grab Alicia and pull her from the basket. Then he snatched up the big sack that had held the balloon and threw it around her shoulders to smother the flames.

Joe yanked the safety pin from the extinguisher and pointed the nozzle at the base of the fire.

Chet, who was next to him, reached for the main valve of the propane tank. Just as Joe squeezed the trigger of the fire extinguisher, releasing a stream of dense white foam, Chet shut off the flow of fuel.

Chet and Joe's quick reactions combined to put a quick end to the fire. Joe continued to spray the area for a few seconds as a precaution. Then he stepped back to take a look around.

Frank was standing next to Alicia, holding the balloon sack tight to her and patting her on the back just to make sure all the flames were out.

Chet rushed over to them. "Alicia, are you all right?" he asked.

Alicia used the back of her hand to wipe her forehead and cheeks. Joe couldn't tell whether she was wiping off sweat or tears or a combination of the two.

"I'm okay," she said. "Just scared out of my mind, that's all. Now I understand why Dad always tells me to wear a jacket. I hate to think what might have happened if I'd been wearing just a T-shirt."

By now a crowd had gathered, drawn by Joe's shout of "You're on fire!" and the unmistakable loud whooshing sound of the fire extinguisher. Alicia's dad appeared and shouldered his way through the circle of onlookers. After making sure Alicia was all right, he went over to the basket and began inspecting the burner and fuel line. Joe and Frank joined him.

"What exactly happened?" Dave Davidson asked.

Joe told him about the little blue flame and pointed out, as best he could, where he had seen it. Alicia's father touched the brass fitting gingerly with a fingertip to make sure it wasn't still hot. Then he pulled a wrench from his pocket and tested the fit.

"Feels tight enough," he said. "Alicia, did you run a full check?"

"All the joints were tight," she reported. "I did a sniff test then *and* before I lit the pilot light."

"Sniff test?" Chet said.

"Just use your nose," Dave Davidson said. "It's the quickest way to find a propane leak. Like this. Everybody back away, just in case." He opened the valve on the propane tank, then put his face down close to the fuel line, sniffing deeply as he followed the line from the tank to the burner. "Not a thing," he said, shutting down the fuel and straightening up.

"If the leak started when the burner was on, maybe it has something to do with the fuel line being hot," Frank suggested.

"Let's check it," Dave Davidson said. He

disconnected the fuel line from the burner, then carefully examined the surface of the inlet and the inside of the brass hex nut.

"That could be it," he said. "Look at this. There's a little dent on the sealing surface here, and a matching one inside the hex nut. When the metal heats up and expands, it could be enough to cause a leak."

"But what could have caused the dents?" Joe asked.

Alicia's dad shrugged his shoulders. "Something hard must have been caught inside when the fitting was tightened," he said. "A little piece of gravel or something. Whatever it was, it's gone now."

While Frank, Joe, and Chet were leaning over to check the fuel line connection with Alicia's dad, she ran a quick preflight-type check on her balloon.

"No other damage to report, Dad," she said. "We were lucky. The worst thing is my jacket's a little bit scorched. Do you think I can still be in the novice event this morning?"

"We've got twenty minutes till takeoff," he said, checking his watch. "There's a spare fuel line in the trailer. If we really hustle, we should just make it."

Just over twenty minutes later, Alicia's ground crew—Frank, Joe, Chet, and her father—stood waving and cheering as the yellow-and-red balloon rose into the air, along with a dozen others. Alicia gave a quick wave, then turned her attention to piloting her craft.

Time to get back to the investigation, Frank thought, wondering if Alicia's mishap could have had anything to do with Dutch Festinger's jammed deflation panel and the extortionist's note. He turned to Dave Davidson and asked, "Was that fitting working all right yesterday?"

"Sure," he replied. "Alicia and I used it for the Hare and Hounds. No problem at all."

"What do you do with your gear at night?" Joe asked.

"Some of the balloonists leave equipment outside in their baskets," he said, "but I don't believe in putting temptation in people's way. We lock everything up in the trailer."

"That means the damage to the fitting must have happened sometime between the Hare and Hounds yesterday and the time we showed up this morning," Frank said.

"I guess so," Dave Davidson said. "Not that it makes much difference. It's nobody's fault, just one of those things. I'll see you fellows later. I'm on chase duty this morning, following Alicia's balloon from the ground." With a friendly nod, he went to his car and drove away.

As soon as his car left, Chet said, "Well, what do you guys think? Another clever act of sabotage?"

Frank tugged at his earlobe as he thought it over. "It could have been," Frank said. "How long would it take to unscrew that hex nut, slip something inside, then retighten it? Less than a minute, but to do it in plain sight would take some nerve. Maybe, like Mr. Davidson just said, it was just one of those things that happens."

"What do you say we fan out and see if we can turn up any more evidence of sabotage while we wait for the extortionist to tip his hand?" Joe said.

Frank nodded, and Chet said, "I'm with you, but how about some breakfast first? I'm starting to work up a pretty good appetite. We're almost past my regular wake-up time now."

"Let's try the hotel," Frank said. "And we can check the office. It's still a little early, but by the time we eat, there should be somebody around."

The IBC office door was closed, and no one answered their knock, but the dining room was open. On a hunch, Frank showed his special pass to the hostess. She said they were welcome to the full buffet breakfast as guests of the IBC.

It was an impressive buffet. There was a

long table down the center of the room lined with trays, bowls, and steaming-hot chafing dishes. The three teenagers took plates and started to dig in. Halfway along, Frank glanced over at Chet's plate. It was piled with scrambled eggs, a slice of ham, two breakfast sausages, a heap of home fries, and toast. Frank was about to make a comment when he realized that his and Joe's plates were at least as full.

They found a vacant table near the windows and settled in. After a few minutes of serious eating, Frank put down his fork and said, "So what's our next move?"

"I'd say Paco has to be our best suspect at this point," Joe said. "At least he's got the motive. I volunteer to keep an eye on him."

"I'll stick with Alicia and her dad," Chet said. "First of all, we should find out whether she or anybody else saw someone near her balloon yesterday after the Hare and Hounds or early this morning. Second, I can just tag along. Since they know almost everybody, I should be able to pick up a lot of useful information."

"Sounds good," Frank said. "And I'll—" He fell silent as he saw Mark Svoboda moving toward their table.

They exchanged greetings. "I've got an invitation for you guys," Svoboda said to Joe and

Frank. "Fred Elwell told me you two are very interested in ballooning. How would you like to ride with me in the fly-in this afternoon?" Turning to Chet, he added, "Sorry, but I only have room for two passengers."

"That's okay," Chet said with a laugh. "After what happened yesterday, I'm taking the day off from active flying duty."

"So are we on?" Svoboda said, turning back to Frank and Joe.

"Definitely," Joe said.

"Why don't you meet me on the front porch of the hotel at two?" he said.

"We'll be there," Frank said. "And thanks. We'll be looking forward to it."

As they finished their breakfast, Joe noticed that Paco Amaya was eating alone at a table across the dining hall. He seemed to be totally absorbed in reading a magazine that was spread out on his table next to a bowl full of cereal, bananas, and strawberries. Joe figured he'd keep an eye on Amaya and time the end of his own meal so he could follow him out of the dining room.

"Don't wait for me, guys," Joe said, nodding casually in the direction of Amaya's table. "I'll be waiting for our friend over there to leave."

Frank and Chet finished up and left Joe at the table nursing his bowl of cereal.

When Amaya got up and left, Joe gave him

a reasonable lead, then sauntered after him. Amaya left the hotel by the main entrance and walked around to a parking lot at the side, where he got into a recreational vehicle with New Mexico license plates. Joe hovered out of sight and waited.

Almost fifteen minutes later, Amaya got out of the RV and strolled down to the field. There he talked casually with half a dozen different people. Joe didn't know any of them by name, but he noted their descriptions, just in case. A few times, Amaya and whoever he was talking to looked over some piece of equipment, but if Amaya committed any sabotage, it was way too subtle for Joe to detect from a distance.

Amaya returned to the hotel and took the wide stairs off the lobby down to the lower level. A big, bare room had been turned into an exposition area, with booths where makers of balloons and balloon equipment showed off their latest products.

Joe followed Amaya through the entrance and glanced at his watch. It was just after nine o'clock. Amaya stopped at a booth halfway down the aisle that featured shiny, complex-looking propane burners. He and the guy staffing the booth began to talk. Joe turned half away and picked up a brochure for a line of digital wristwatches that were also altimeters, variometers, barometers, and thermometers and had built-in compasses. As he read the long list of other functions, Joe began to wonder if all this was a waste of time.

Amaya finished his conversation and glanced around. Joe edged back into the shadows made by the booth. As he did, he heard a man talking in a low voice with a note of urgency. He quickly realized the voice was coming from the other side of the drapes behind the booth where he was standing.

Joe strained to pick up the conversation.

"I know I'm late," the man said. "But I will definitely have the money for you on Monday. . . . Yes, I absolutely guarantee it."

Joe realized he was overhearing half of a phone conversation.

"Yes, that's right. I *will* have it—all hundred thousand of it."

Chapter 7

ONE HUNDRED THOUSAND DOLLARS? Joe couldn't believe what he had just heard. The mysterious voice had just promised to deliver on Monday the exact amount of money that the extortion note demanded. Was it possible that Joe had just stumbled onto the extortionist?

There was a click as the man hung up the telephone. Joe stepped forward, picked up another brochure, and pretended to be absorbed in reading it. The man, who quickly walked out from behind the drapes, nearly bumped into Joe.

It was Harris Scott, the designer-builder of *Earthquest.*

Scott's face seemed redder than usual. He stopped dead in his tracks and stared at Joe for a couple of beats. Then, with a mumbled apology, he pushed past Joe and hurried off down the corridor.

Was Scott their man? He certainly had a reason to need a lot of money. Joe wanted to follow him and try to find out, but someone called out his name from behind. He peeked back over his shoulder. It was Paco Amaya.

"Hey, Joe, how are you doing?" Amaya said, coming up and clapping Joe on the shoulder. "I still can't get over what you did yesterday. Too bad it had to be Dutch Festinger you rescued."

"I know," Joe said, wondering if Amaya had forgotten that Chet was with Festinger. "Has he always been like this?"

"Pretty much," Amaya said. "When he first showed up on the circuit, I tried to help him, show him the ropes, you know? All I got for thanks was him telling people I was trying to sabotage his equipment. That's a laugh. The only thing that keeps that turkey in the air is his topflight crew chief.

"I'm glad I ran into you," Amaya continued. "How would you and your brother and your friend like to come over at noon for a lunch of real New Mexican cooking?"

"Sounds great," Joe said. "Come by

where?" He didn't want to let on that he'd followed Amaya earlier and knew all about his RV and where it was parked.

Amaya gave him directions, then returned to the exposition. Joe went off in search of Frank. After a few minutes, he found him out on the field.

"I was just coming to look for you," Frank said. "What's up?"

Joe quickly told him about Scott's phone call. "If it's a coincidence, it's a pretty wild one," he said. "We know that *Earthquest* is costing him a lot of money. We know he's mad at the Lift people for not agreeing to sponsor him. What if he decided to lay his hands on a lot of money *and* get back at the Lift company with one stroke?"

"He could definitely be our man," Frank said. "Nice work, Joe."

"Hey, I stumbled on it," Joe said.

"It never hurts to be lucky," Frank said.

"Now all we need is some physical evidence to connect him to the notes or the 'accidents,' " Joe said.

They decided to head over to the IBC office to see if they could piece together anything more about the extortion note. As they climbed the steps to the long covered porch of the hotel, Joe told Frank about Amaya's lunch invitation.

"That's great," Frank said. "It'll give us a chance to ask him a few casual questions. I just had a long talk with one of Dutch's ground crew. He thinks he saw Paco near the balloon yesterday afternoon, but he's not sure if it was before or after the envelope was inflated."

"Do you think Paco could be working with Scott?" Joe said.

"Anything's possible," Frank said.

Inside the office, they found Elwell standing near the window. When they joined him, he urgently handed them a piece of paper and said in an undertone, "Look what I just got."

Frank took the paper, unfolded it, and read. Then he handed it to Joe.

" 'Alicia Davidson was lucky,' " Joe read. " 'The next one might not be. Get the money ready. Small bills only. Await further instructions. And don't call in any cops.' "

"Same paper and type font," Frank said. "How did you get it?"

"Marie found it slipped under the door a little while ago," Elwell replied. "After that, I decided to leave the door open. That way, nobody sneaks up on us."

"Can't blame you," Joe said. "What do you think?"

"I don't know," Elwell said. "I'll have to see what Max says. That's two accidents and two notes in two days. This guy is definitely willing to carry through on his threats. I really don't like knuckling under, but . . ."

"We're trying to fix it so you don't have to," Frank said.

"Have you come up with anything else?" Elwell asked. Both Frank and Joe knew it was too early to mention their suspicions—at least not until they had some hard evidence.

Frank spoke for them both. "We're still collecting leads. For example, where these notes came from. Are there any other laser printers around here? Maybe in the hotel office?"

"Not that I know of," Elwell replied. "We had to bring this one in ourselves. It turns out that the Wilderland still uses an impact printer because they have to make a lot of carbon copies. Are you saying the note might have been typed in this office?"

"It's a possibility," Frank said. "We need to check with Marie Thibault to find out who might have used the computer."

"Go ahead," Elwell said with a wave of his hand.

Marie Thibault was working at the terminal as the Hardys strode to the back of the office. She turned with a start when Joe's shadow crossed the monitor screen.

"Oh, hi, it's you," she said, glancing up. "How's it going? Are you guys getting anywhere?"

"We don't know yet," Frank said. "But nobody's supposed to know what we're up to."

"Oops, sorry. Not another word out of me," Thibault said with a sheepish grin. She slid a finger across her lips, as if zipping them closed. "Can I help you with anything?"

"Yes," Frank said. "I'd just like to print out a few sample sentences on the computer here."

"Sure, just let me exit this file." A few mouse clicks later, she pushed back her chair and said, "It's all yours."

Frank sat down and quickly typed the words *Small bills, Alicia,* and *call in any cops.* After formatting the text in fourteen-point Helvetica, he gave the print command. The laser printer, on a table next to the wall, began to hum.

Joe went to retrieve the page from the printer. He checked it over, then handed it to Frank. "We should match it against the original notes, but it sure looks the same to me," Joe said in a low voice.

"Did I do anything wrong?" Marie Thibault asked.

"Not at all," Frank assured her. "We were just wondering who uses the computer besides you."

She blinked a couple of times. "Well, let's see . . ." she said. "There's Zoë and Tiffany. They help out with the paperwork. And Marjorie, who does the accounts. And Mr. Elwell uses it now and then when he needs to write letters or reports. That's about it."

"How about any of the balloonists?" Joe asked.

"Well, sure," Thibault replied. "I thought you meant as a regular thing. If somebody comes in and wants to write a quick note or something, the way you just did, I almost always let them, unless we're swamped with work. Do you think that's okay?"

"Sure, no problem," Frank said. "Do you have any idea who used it, either yesterday or this morning?"

"Things were pretty hectic in here, getting all the press materials ready," she said. "I know Paco Amaya did, and so did Alicia Davidson. She came by just before I closed up to get ready for the dinner. There were a few others, too."

"How about Harris Scott?" Frank asked.

"Harris uses it almost every day," she said. "He's always writing letters trying to get sponsorship for his around-the-world flight. He was here yesterday. And this morning, too, for maybe five minutes."

"What about Mark Svoboda?" Frank asked.

Marie Thibault shook her head. "Definitely not him," she said.

"Anyone else?" Joe asked.

"Jan Simonsen was here," she said. "And

Mike Carluccio. He's piloting the Lift balloon. That's it, I think."

"Is the office ever left open with nobody here?" Joe asked.

"A lot of times I'm the only one here," she replied. "If I have to leave, I usually lock up. But if I'm going to be gone for just a minute, I might not. It depends. I'm practically always here, anyway," she added.

Frank and Joe asked Marie Thibault a few more questions but didn't get any more significant information. They thanked her and went outside to look for Chet to tell him about Amaya's lunch invitation.

"Looks like Harris Scott has motive *and* opportunity," Joe said as they made their way through the crowds to the fenced-in takeoff area.

"I'm not sure motive's going to help us much," Frank said. "The hundred thousand dollars is motive enough for anybody who's not afraid to steal. What we have to look for is someone who doesn't mind risking other people's lives to get it."

The crowds were a lot thinner inside the enclosure. They found Chet with Alicia, near the Davidsons' car. The wicker basket and the folded balloon were still sitting in the trailer.

"Hey, guess who took first in the novice

event," Chet said when he saw Frank and Joe. "Alicia."

"Congratulations," the Hardys said at the same time.

Alicia laughed. "Thanks," she said. "We're throwing a little picnic to celebrate. Would you like to join us?"

"I wish we could, but we've already got a lunch date with Paco Amaya," Joe said. "And this afternoon, we're doing the fly-in with Mark Svoboda."

"That's a great event," Alicia said. She explained how a fly-in worked. All the balloonists drove to the launch spot of their choice, then tried to fly back to the base. "The spectators love it. They get to watch the balloons coming in from lots of different directions at different altitudes."

"Who wins?" Joe asked.

"Everybody who makes it back," she said. "That's one of the nice things about it. No huge prize to fight over. No hard feelings."

Just then Joe spotted a rider buzzing across the field on a purple trail bike. "That looks like Paco," he said. The rider was wearing a full helmet, but the visor was up.

"It sure is," Frank said. He raised his hand and waved. Amaya waved back, then rode over to them.

"Hi, guys," he said. "I was looking for you.

I have to run a couple of errands, but I left the camper unlocked. Why don't you meet me over there in a few minutes?" Before Frank or Joe could answer, Amaya twisted the throttle and took off.

"I need to go up to the hotel for a few minutes," Alicia said. "Chet, would you mind helping me get the stuff together for the picnic? The cooler and all the supplies are in the trunk. I'll be right back."

"Sure," Chet said. Alicia grabbed her shoulder bag and walked off toward the hotel. Once she was out of earshot, Frank took the opportunity to fill Chet in about the new extortion note and Harris Scott's phone call that Joe had overheard.

"Harris Scott?" Chet said. "I can't believe it. He seems like such a dedicated guy."

"Sometimes there's a fine line between dedicated and fanatic," Joe said. "Fanatics are the kind of people who'll stop at nothing to get what they want. Harris Scott may be one of them."

"I'll see what I can find out about him from Alicia," Chet said.

"See if you can get her talking about some of the other competitors, too," Frank said. "You never know what you might turn up."

"Okay," Chet replied. "But don't you think

it's about time we let her know what we're up to? I'm sure she could help out."

"Sorry, Chet," Frank said. "Elwell and Arneson asked us to keep this investigation quiet. And that's what we've got to do, at least for now."

As soon as Alicia returned, Joe and Frank set off for Amaya's, leaving Chet to help out with the Davidsons' picnic setup.

They were approaching Amaya's RV when Dutch Festinger seemed to appear out of nowhere. He jogged in front of them, turned, planted his feet, and said, "Hold it, you two. I want you to tell your friends that my balloon is under constant guard."

"Whatever you say, Dutch," Joe said. "Which friends would you be talking about?"

"You heard me. Your friends," Festinger repeated, poking his forefinger at Joe's chest for emphasis. "Tell them not to interfere, or they'll be very sorry."

"You're making a mistake, accusing—" Frank began to say. But Festinger had already stalked away.

"Can you believe that guy?" Joe said. "He's been watching way too many bad movies."

When they reached Amaya's camper, Frank and Joe saw that their host had put out a table in the shade. It was already set for lunch. The door of the camper stood ajar. Joe went up to it and called inside, "Hey, Paco, we're here. Time for lunch."

There was no answer. Slightly uneasy, Joe stepped inside and looked around. Plates, utensils, and food were neatly arranged on the counter of the cooking area. From a pot simmering on the stove came a delicious, spicy aroma, which filled the small space.

Then Joe spotted something strange. Dangling from the cabinet over the sink was a length of rope, tied in a hangman's noose. There was a large iron nail stuck through a piece of paper and into the rope. The paper had a short message written on it in big red block letters: "Amaya está muerto."

A shiver went up Joe's spine. Spanish wasn't his strongest subject at school, but he remembered enough to understand that phrase.

It meant "Amaya is dead."

Chapter 8

"FRANK," JOE SAID, "there's something in here you ought to take a look at."

Joe's eyes were locked on the noose, which lent a deadly, ominous air to the neatly kept living area. Frank stepped inside the camper, and it rocked slightly. The rope also swayed gently from side to side.

Frank came in and stopped a couple of feet from the cabinet.

"We just saw Paco five minutes ago," Joe said without turning around. "You don't really think—"

"I think somebody's trying to send Paco a message," Frank said.

"Not exactly a friendly hello," Joe said.

"More like a threat or a warning," Frank said.

Joe started looking around the camper for anything else out of the ordinary while Frank carefully examined the noose, making sure not to touch it.

"Nothing unusual about this cord," Frank said. He figured if this was an amateur job, they might find some fingerprints on the note. It wasn't going to help them find the culprit in the short run, but it was worth saving for evidence later.

Frank stared at the handwriting on the note. The six letters that spelled *dead* in Spanish—*M-U-E-R-T-O*—were printed in block letters with a thick red marker. Whoever wrote it obviously did his best to make them look as ordinary as possible. Still, there was something funny about those letters. Frank couldn't pinpoint it at first. Then he realized that the two *E*'s were a very distinctive shape.

"Joe," he said. "Take a look at those capital *E*'s. They're shaped a little like backward threes."

Joe stared at the note. "Pretty uncommon," he said.

"And if I'm not mistaken," Frank said, "much more European than American."

"Funny thing about that," Joe said. "Didn't we just run into a certain balloonist from Holland who's already picked one fight with Paco? Sounds like a pretty good fit."

"Maybe a little *too* good," Frank said.

"I was thinking it's just Dutch's way of getting back at Paco," Joe said. "Dutch blames Paco for his accident. That's it."

"I think it smells like a setup," Frank said. "And anyway, where does it all tie into the extortion plot?" They both heard the *blatt* of a two-cycle engine winding down in the background.

"Look at it this way," Joe said as the sound of the trail bike moved steadily closer. "These guys, with their constant bickering, are the perfect smoke screen for whoever the extortionist is. Every time they have another blowup, we get involved, and that takes us off the trail."

"But what if one of them—" Frank didn't have a chance to finish his sentence because the trail bike had already come buzzing up and pulled to a stop just outside the door. Amaya bounded into the camper and tossed his black helmet down on a seat.

"Sorry I took so long," Amaya said. "I—"

He noticed the noose dangling from the cabinet, and the rest of his words caught in his throat. Then his eyes narrowed, and Frank thought he saw a vein pop out in the man's temple.

"What is going on here?" Amaya said. "Is this somebody's idea of a joke?"

"We found it when we got here," Joe said.

"It has to be that jerk Festinger," Amaya said. "Who else would pull a stunt like this?"

Amaya's hand lashed out, and an instant later, the noose, with its threatening message, lay crumpled on the floor. Well, Frank thought, Paco Amaya's fingerprints will definitely be on the note now. The question was who else's might be.

"Paco," Joe said. "Any chance you left the camper door open when you left?"

Amaya looked at Joe. "Open?" he repeated. "No, of course not. I pulled it closed."

"But it was unlocked," Joe said.

Amaya shrugged. "Like I told you guys, it wasn't locked. I never lock it if I'm only going to be gone for a few minutes. I hate fumbling with keys every time. It's the same with my bike. When I park it, I leave the key in it."

"Nobody steals it?" Joe asked.

"Not yet." The corner of Amaya's mouth twitched in what Joe thought was amusement. "Crooks leave it alone because they think it must be a trap. And honest people don't take other people's property."

"Do a lot of people know about this habit of leaving things unlocked?" Frank asked. He was pretty sure he knew the answer. The world of competitive ballooning was such a small, tight-knit group that he would be surprised if word hadn't gotten around.

With another shrug, Amaya said, "I've heard that people talk about it, but what do

I care? I have my own way of doing things, that's all."

He stepped over to the stove, lifted the lid from the pot, and gave the contents a stir. "Why don't you have a seat outside?" he said. "Give yourselves some room to breathe. I should have lunch on the table in about three minutes."

Joe and Frank went out to the table under the trees and sat down. After a short silence, Joe said, "Just about anybody could have seen Paco ride away, then come over to check to see if the camper was unlocked."

"Maybe they overheard him tell us it was unlocked," Frank added.

"Whoever it was must have had the noose in his pocket all ready," Joe said. "Otherwise, there wouldn't have been time to go get it, tie the knot, hang it up, and get out of there before we entered."

"Which means they've been following Paco around," Frank said. "And maybe us, too."

"You know what I just thought?" Joe said under his breath as Amaya stepped out of his RV, carrying a platter of steaming enchiladas. "What if the guy strung up that noose and then decided to slip a little surprise into the sauce that was bubbling away on the stove?"

The enchiladas were delicious, but Amaya became increasingly sullen as the meal wore on. It didn't help when Joe mentioned that they were doing the fly-in with Mark Svoboda. By the end of the meal, Amaya was staring silently at the table, seemingly not hearing a word of their conversation.

Frank and Joe helped clear the table and wash up. Then they thanked Amaya for lunch and left. As they walked away, Frank said, "I wonder what got into him."

"He was fighting mad when he found that noose," Joe said. "Then he got quieter and quieter. I wonder if he's just plain scared."

"Well, we're not talking about a Valentine's Day card," Frank pointed out. "This sport is high-risk enough without having to worry about backstabbers. It's got to be pretty nerve-wracking, floating up there at twenty-five hundred feet in a basket not knowing who your enemies are."

"Tell me about it," Joe said.

Frank thought for a moment. "I guess the question now is, do we take Paco off our suspect list?"

"Why wouldn't we?" Joe said.

"He could have put the noose there," Frank said, "just to take suspicion away from himself."

"Why would he do that? Unless . . ." Joe said, thinking out loud. "Unless, of course, he's the extortionist and sees right through our cover."

"Why do you think he invited us to lunch?"

Frank replied. "Weren't you a little surprised about that?"

"It *would* make perfect sense if he was planning for us to find that noose," Joe said.

By now they had reached the front of the hotel. It was a short wait until Mark Svoboda showed up. He led them over to the entrance to the balloon staging area, where they all showed their passes. They followed Svoboda over to a red van. He glanced impatiently at his large, complex-looking wristwatch and said, "My ground crew should be here any minute. I want to get an early start. There's a launch site I checked out yesterday that's perfect for the wind today."

"Wind?" Frank said, peering up at the low ceiling of clouds. "It feels pretty calm to me."

"Maybe down here," Svoboda replied. "But I sent up some pibals a while back, and we've got variable winds starting at about five hundred feet."

"What's a 'pie-ball'?" Joe asked.

Svoboda actually cracked a smile. "Pibals," he repeated. "Short for 'pilot balloons.' They're just little helium balloons, the kind you have at a party. You let them go and watch to see what the winds do to them at different altitudes."

When Svoboda's crew arrived, he introduced them as Sue and Ron, and they all got in the van for the trip to the launch site. Ron drove. After forty-five minutes he pulled off the road beside an open, grassy area. Frank looked around and realized that they were just a few miles from Bayport. Would they end up passing right over the town?

Frank and Joe helped carry the basket from the rear of the van, then returned for the inflator fan while Ron and Sue laid out the balloon envelope and Mark Svoboda went through his preflight check. Soon the balloon, which was a checkerboard of blue and white squares, was blown up and ready for takeoff. Frank and Joe joined Svoboda in the basket.

"The radio was on and off again yesterday," Svoboda told his crew. "Don't be too worried if we lose contact. We'll see you back at the field in an hour or so."

Svoboda reached up and pulled the lanyard for a five-second burn, paused, and did it again. Frank watched the ground smoothly recede, then looked around and gave Joe a big grin. This was something else.

Within a couple of minutes, the balloon reached the level of the overcast and continued to rise. Suddenly it was as if they were floating through a dense fog. Frank could feel tiny water droplets on his face. Less than a minute later, just as suddenly, the balloon broke through the low-hanging clouds into a magical region of blue skies and bright sunlight, with what appeared to be a heaving sea of gray-white fluff below them.

Frank watched the cloud layer with growing puzzlement. Finally he asked, "Did we stop moving?"

Svoboda looked up from his instruments and shook his head. "It just looks that way," he said. "We're moving, all right. At a pretty good clip, too. But we're going at exactly the same speed as the cloud cover, so you don't have any sense of motion. There's no reference point. If you got a glimpse of the ground, you'd know we're moving."

He studied the complex read-out on his watch, scribbled some numbers on his clip-board, then picked up a map and shook its folds loose.

"Are you navigating strictly on instruments?" Frank asked.

"Yep," Svoboda said, peering at his map.

"That must be tricky," Joe said.

"Let's just say it's a whole lot easier when you can see landmarks on the ground," Svoboda replied. "But no problem. You guys just sit back and enjoy the ride. I'll worry about driving the bus."

Frank leaned his elbows on the railing of the basket and gazed out across the sky. He imagined drifting endlessly in a place where time had slowed almost to a stop. It came as a shock when their host said, "We should be near the Wilderland by now. We're going to go down for a look-see."

Svoboda opened his deflation panel briefly, and soon they were in the clouds again. Frank waited for his first sight of the ground. But when they broke through the cloud cover, all he saw was a rippled field of gray stretching in all directions. He knew it wasn't the ground, but it took him a few seconds to realize that he was looking at open water. There was no land anywhere in sight.

"Whoa—" Svoboda said. He took a long look at his compass, shook it a few times, then leaned over the side to peer down at the water. Then he stood up straight again and scanned the horizon in both directions for several seconds. "I don't believe this," he said, shaking his head.

"Any idea where we are?" Joe asked.

"Your guess is as good as mine," Svoboda said. "I'd say we're somewhere out over the ocean—with a busted compass and not a whole lot of fuel left."

Chapter 9

JOE COULDN'T BELIEVE IT, either. If they had to ditch over the ocean, the balloon might float for a while, but the basket would sink in seconds. A quick look around confirmed what he suspected. There were no life vests on board.

"Suppose we went east instead of west," Frank said. "That means this is either the Sound or the Atlantic Ocean."

"So all we do is head back in the direction we came from," Joe said, "and we should be back over dry land in no time. . . ."

Svoboda stared at Joe quizzically, as if he wasn't sure whether to take the remark seriously.

"First of all," the balloonist said, "we have a broken compass, so we don't have any idea which direction we came from, do we? And as long as we can't see the coastline, it doesn't matter where we head—it could just as easily be heading in the *wrong* direction, which puts us even farther out to sea. By the time we figure out we're wrong, we're out of fuel.

"For all we know," Svoboda continued, "we could be right in the middle of a landing pattern for a major airport."

The water was closer now. Svoboda turned on the burner for a few seconds, then sent out a radio message identifying them and explaining their situation. "We could be out of range, or this thing might not be working again, like yesterday," he said. "But it's worth a try."

They drifted for another fifteen minutes or more, with each of them searching in a different direction. Frank was the first to spot something.

"Looks like that could be a fishing boat," he said, pointing to a dot in the distance. "Maybe we could scan the radio band and try picking them up."

"*If* they have their radio on," Joe said. "And *if* we can find their frequency, and *if* our radio is transmitting."

"Let's just go ask them," Svoboda said. He took a tissue from his pocket, wadded it loosely, tossed it out of the basket, and watched it drift downward. "Okay," he said.

"We've got a breeze headed their way at about four hundred feet."

He gave another quick tug on the red rope that controlled the deflation panel, letting out a small amount of hot air. Joe didn't feel any change, but within thirty seconds he noticed the waves were starting to look bigger. They were definitely losing altitude. He could also tell they were moving toward the boat.

"How're we going to talk to those guys?" Joe asked.

"You'll see," Svoboda said.

By now, Joe could make out details on the boat. It was a sleek sport fisherman, at least forty-five feet, he figured, with a flying bridge and all the latest radar equipment for deep-sea fishing. Joe knew that boats like that sometimes went on overnight charters more than one hundred miles offshore. Could they be that far out?

The boat was drifting with four lines out, two on each side, and a slick of chum—chopped-up fish flesh and innards—spreading around it. They were waiting for a shark to bite.

There were half a dozen people clustered in the boat's stern, and as the balloon approached, one of them pointed up. There was a brief pinpoint of light as one of them took a snapshot and the flashbulb went off.

The balloon drifted lower still, until it was no more than twenty feet off the ocean. Svoboda kept shifting between the burner lanyard and the deflation cord. He was maintaining such a delicate balance that Joe imagined the balloon might start going up again if he so much as tossed his pocket change overboard.

They were nearly over the boat. Svoboda leaned out, cupped his hands around his mouth, and yelled, "Which way to shore? Our compass is broken."

On the bridge, a man in a battered captain's cap checked his instruments, then pointed to his right. "That way—north-northwest. You want me to radio the Coast Guard?" he added.

"No, thanks," Svoboda yelled. "But could you call my ground crew on VHF frequency one twenty-three point three? Tell them you saw us. We're balloon Nine Three Nine Echo."

"That's VHF one twenty-three point three, balloon Nine Three Nine Echo," the captain shouted back, just to make sure he had it right.

"That's it," Svoboda said.

"Okay," the captain said with a wave. "Good flying."

"Thanks for your help, skipper," Svoboda yelled, then gave the balloon another quick blast with the burner.

As the balloon gained altitude again, Joe muttered to Frank, " 'Good flying'? How about 'Happy landings'?"

* * *

Half an hour later, as they neared the shoreline, the clouds began to break up. Joe tried to fit what he was seeing on the ground to his mental map of the area. It was surprisingly hard to do from the air. Even when he saw what looked like familiar landmarks—a shopping mall here, a ball field there—he still wasn't sure exactly where they were.

"We should be there in a few minutes," Svoboda said. "And none too soon, as far as the fuel supply goes."

"Have you ever had any problems with this compass before?" Frank asked.

"Do you think I would have flown on a day like this if I had?" the balloonist replied.

Frank bent over and took a close look at the instrument panel. "A magnetic compass is a pretty simple device," he said. "There's not a lot that can go wrong with it. And this one *is* registering. It just happens to be way off. I wonder . . ."

Joe watched Frank get down on one knee and turn his head around to peer up at the underside of the instruments.

Frank grabbed something, pulled it down, and then straightened up so suddenly that the edge of the instrument panel grazed his forehead. "Look what I found," he said. He held out his hand. In his palm was a colorful plastic model of a hot-air balloon, about two inches long. The letters *N-M-A* were printed across the balloon.

"I don't get it," Joe started to say.

Frank flipped over the model to reveal the magnet cemented to the back. "It's for putting notes on your refrigerator," he said. "*Not* for sticking up next to a magnetic compass. No wonder we went off course."

"You know," Joe said slowly, "I can't help thinking I've seen a magnet like that before. . . ."

As Joe spoke, Svoboda snatched the refrigerator-door magnet from Frank, hefted it in his hand, and turned it over a few times.

"I don't know if you have, but *I* have," he said. "I know those initials. They stand for New Mexico Aeronauts. And the only NMA member at this meet is Paco Amaya. That scum. I should have known he'd try something."

"I wouldn't be too quick to jump to conclusions," Frank said.

"He's right, Mark," Joe said, "I believe the situation's a little more complicated than you might think."

"Why don't you two just stay out of it," Svoboda said. "I can take care of my business without your help."

Joe wanted to say something more to calm him down, but he decided not to push it. He'd rather see Svoboda concentrate on flying the balloon and making a smooth landing than start another argument about who was trying to sabotage whom.

They spent the rest of the ride in awkward silence. A couple of minutes after the Wilderland Resort came into view, Svoboda overflew the field and set down on the far edge. When the basket hit the ground, it tipped over and was dragged a dozen yards before it came to a stop. By the time Joe and Frank untangled themselves, climbed out, and got to their feet, the red van was braking to a stop next to them. Sue and Ron jumped out and hurried over.

"What happened?" Sue demanded. "You had us pretty worried."

"I'll tell you later," said Svoboda, who had executed a quick roll to a standing position. "You wrap things up. I'll be right back. I'm going to pay a little visit to Paco Amaya."

Joe and Frank teamed up to help stretch the wrinkles out of the balloon. As they worked, Frank asked, "If you were about to pull a dirty trick on somebody, would you be extra careful to do it so it could be tied directly to you?"

"Hey, great artists sign their paintings, don't they?" Joe replied. "And what do you usually find around a painting?"

"A frame," Frank said. "But who's doing the framing and why?"

"I'm beginning to think we're not going to

know the answers to those questions until we find the extortionist," Joe said.

Stowing the balloon didn't take long. As the Hardys helped lift the basket into the van, Frank asked, "Do you always keep this stuff in the van? I notice a lot of people leave their equipment sitting out."

Ron nodded. "Mark's very particular," he said. "He doesn't want anybody messing with his gear. So we keep the whole rig under lock and key except when we're actually getting it ready for a flight."

"Do you happen to know when the compass was last checked?" Joe asked.

Ron stopped to stare at him. "The compass? Today, around one o'clock. We took the basket out of the van to make sure everything was ready for the fly-in. We don't ever want to get to a launch site and find out we're missing an important piece of gear. The compass was working fine then."

"Between then and the time you locked it in the van again, was there anyone who came near the basket?" Joe asked.

"Nobody at all," Ron said.

Svoboda was back in time to hear this exchange. "You're forgetting something," he told Ron. "You and Sue went back to the hotel for another pair of gloves. While you were gone, all the gear was sitting out in plain sight."

"But, Mark, you were here," Sue protested.

"Not the whole time," he said. "I left for about five minutes to chat with a couple of people I hadn't seen in a while. It was pretty stupid of me, now that I think about it."

"And you didn't notice anybody hanging around your stuff?" Frank asked.

"I couldn't see from where I was," Svoboda said. "The only thing I did see was Paco riding by on his motorbike."

"You're sure?" Joe asked. "Did you see his face?"

Svoboda hesitated. "He had his sun visor down, but I'd know that purple bike of his anywhere. You can hear it a mile away."

As if on cue, Joe heard the buzz of a two-cycle engine coming slowly down the row of balloons. He stepped out from behind the van and shaded his eyes. Sure enough, it was Amaya.

Frank stepped up next to Joe. "Oh, great," he muttered. "Batten down the hatches. We're in for a storm."

Amaya steered his machine over to the edge of the grassy lane and parked it. After leaving his helmet on the saddle, he walked up to Svoboda and said, "I hear you had some trouble."

"You hear things pretty quickly," Svoboda said. "I wonder why."

Joe exchanged a quick glance with Frank.

The two of them moved in closer in case there was trouble.

"I keep my ear to the ground because I have to," Amaya said. "There are too many people around here messing in other people's business."

Svoboda raised his fist. For an instant, it looked as if he was going to let Amaya have it. Joe was ready to break it up. But instead of throwing a punch, Svoboda slowly opened his fingers to reveal the NMA balloon magnet.

"I found this near my compass," he said. "It does belong to you, doesn't it?"

Amaya became very still as he stared down at the magnet.

"Don't tell me," Svoboda said in a mocking tone. "You had a break-in at your camper just this morning, and somebody stole your refrigerator magnet—so they could screw up my compass with it and make it look like you did it."

"There wasn't anybody—" Amaya started to say. "Hey, wait a second. The only people who were in my camper were these guys," he said, jerking his thumb toward Frank and Joe.

Then Amaya turned on Joe and said, "So what's your alibi? That magnet was stuck on the fridge before lunch. I show up, and you guys are snooping around my rig. The magnet turns up missing, and then somebody uses it to send Svoboda on a fishing trip."

"You must be joking, Paco," Joe said. "Why would we mess with his compass and then jump right in his basket and go for a ride?"

"Just answer my question," Amaya said, stepping up in Joe's face. "And come to think of it, how come every place you two guys show up, there's a fight or a fire or a jimmied piece of equipment?"

"Calm down, Paco," Joe said. "We're trying to figure out the same thing."

"Well, maybe it's about time you guys stop asking all the questions and start answering a few," Amaya said. "What's the deal, huh? What are you up to?"

Amaya was practically yelling now, and he was so close to Joe's face that Joe could smell his breath.

"All right, Paco," Joe said. "Just cool it." Then Joe laid his hands on Amaya's shoulders and gave him a big smile. "We're just as upset as—"

"That's it," Amaya growled as he threw Joe's hands off. "Get off me!" He shoved Joe hard in the chest. "I've had enough of you."

Joe stumbled back, regained his balance, and moved in on Amaya. "Watch who you're shoving around," Joe said. But before he could get in another word, Amaya made a quick half-turn, cocked his right elbow, and buried his left fist in the pit of Joe's stomach.

Chapter 10

IT WAS A SOLID PUNCH, and when it landed, Joe let out an involuntary grunt—*"Huh!"* He doubled over, the wind knocked out of him, gasping for air.

As Joe clutched his midsection, Amaya unloaded a left cross aimed at the side of Joe's neck. Joe went deeper into his crouch and ducked Amaya's second punch.

Then Joe mustered his strength, drove forward at Amaya's knees, and straightened up to his full height. Amaya, caught off balance, did a half-flip over Joe's shoulders and crashed to the ground, stunned. He struggled to his feet and charged again, arms windmilling.

Joe waited until Amaya was nearly on him.

Then he took a quick step to the left, stretching his right leg out. Joe gave Amaya a push, and the balloonist tripped and went sprawling again.

By now a small crowd had gathered. Two guys Joe didn't know grabbed Amaya by the arms, helped him to his feet, and held him back. They were trying to talk him out of another attack.

A three-person video crew appeared, wearing matching jackets with a network logo on them. The camera lens swiveled in Joe's direction. He could just imagine an anchorperson saying, "A disturbance broke out today at the hot-air balloon meet being held at the Wilderland Resort . . ." while Joe's scowling face appeared on the screen. He'd have a lot of explaining to do after this one.

Alicia pushed her way through the crowd and stood facing Joe. "Joe, you should leave Paco alone," she said.

"Hey, hold on," Joe retorted. "The guy punched me in the stomach. He tried to slug me a few more times, too, but I managed to get out of the way. What do you expect me to do, send him flowers?"

Alicia looked confused. "Well, you must have done something to set him off."

"I didn't do anything," Joe insisted. "I was just trying to calm him down."

"Joe's telling the truth, Alicia," Frank said, stepping forward. "Paco and Mark were talking, when Paco decided he had a beef with Joe and went after him."

"You!" Amaya shouted at Frank. He struggled to get free of the two men who were holding him. "You're just as much to blame!"

Amaya looked around at the crowd. "Yesterday those little creeps made Dutch Festinger think I was pulling dirty tricks on him," he said. "This morning they hung a noose in in my camper and 'discovered' it when they showed up. Then they stole a magnet off my refrigerator and used it to wreck Svoboda's compass during the fly-in. Doesn't anybody see what they're up to?"

Joe couldn't believe it. Was this the same guy who had made enchiladas for them just a few hours before? Worse, Joe could see from the faces in the crowd that most people were on Amaya's side. Hadn't any of them seen Amaya haul off and slug him?

Joe saw Chet pull Alicia aside and start to talk to her earnestly. She glanced over in Joe's direction a few times. At least Alicia would be on their side . . .

Dutch Festinger pushed his way to the front of the crowd. "I want to know, who are these two?" he said. "What are they doing here? None of us has seen them before, they know nothing about ballooning, but suddenly they are everywhere. And everywhere they go, there are more problems. Tomorrow is the Lift Challenge. We cannot afford any more trouble. I say we ban them from the meet."

A couple of balloonists in the crowd nodded in agreement. Joe wanted to tell them the real story, but he knew he couldn't. Wasn't anyone going to stick up for them?

"Where's Mark Svoboda?" Frank said. "He'll tell you what really happened."

There was a short silence. Joe looked around the circle of faces. Mark Svoboda's wasn't one of them.

Fred Elwell's voice rose up from the back of the crowd. "Okay, folks, coming through," he said. "I've got something to say."

Elwell came up and stood between Joe and Frank. "First, I want to say that I know these boys personally," he said, "and I can guarantee that they are not doing anything underhanded. Just put that out of your minds." He paused and looked at Dutch Festinger, then at Paco Amaya. Neither of them met his gaze.

"Second," Elwell continued, "we'll be passing out the maps for the FIFO event on the front steps of the hotel in fifteen minutes. So if you want to take part, be sure to be there. Now, let's all get back to what we're good at—ballooning."

After clapping both Joe and Frank on the back, Elwell made his way hastily through the crowd and walked away. After a few moments, the crowd began to disperse. Both Amaya and Festinger walked off without so much as a backward glance at the Hardys. Joe rubbed the back of his neck, which was a little sore from flipping Amaya onto the ground.

When Chet and Alicia came over, Chet asked, "So what was it all about?"

"More dirty tricks," Joe said. He explained how the magnet next to Svoboda's compass was enough to send them on a little detour out over the Atlantic Ocean.

When he was done, Alicia said, "I'd better finish loading our gear on the trailer. We're not in the FIFO this time."

"We'll give you a hand," Frank offered. As they walked across the field, he asked, "What is a FIFO, anyway?"

"It sounds like a good name for a poodle, doesn't it?" Alicia said with a chuckle. "It really stands for 'fly in, fly on.' Everybody gets a map with a spot marked on it. First, you steer your balloon to that target. When you get there, you drop your map marked with another target that you've chosen to fly onto. Your score depends on how close you get to both targets."

The Davidsons' pickup truck, with a brand-new front tire, and trailer were just ahead. "That's weird," Alicia said, walking a little faster. "I'm sure I fastened the balloon bag shut. Chet and I were about to load it on the trailer."

The mouth of the bag was open, revealing the colorful fabric of the rolled-up balloon. Alicia went over and examined something inside the bag for several seconds. Then she said, "Hey, somebody tried to cut the deflation cord!"

Alicia pulled out a section of the cord, which was really a webbed strap, and held it up. It was slashed almost all the way through. A couple of good tugs, and the strap would have broken.

"Are you sure it was okay earlier?" Frank asked.

"Of course I am," Alicia replied. "I wouldn't have missed something like that."

Frank and Joe both saw instantly what that meant. Paco Amaya and Dutch Festinger had been over near Mark Svoboda's van when Alicia's deflation cord was sliced. Only one of their suspects—Harris Scott—hadn't been part of that crowd.

When they finished stowing the gear, Alicia said, "I'd better tell my dad about this right away. He's at some kind of committee meeting over at the hotel. He's going to be furious."

"We'll walk you over," Frank said. "We're going that way ourselves."

"To talk to Harris Scott," Joe said.

Chet looked puzzled but didn't say anything.

All over the field, ground crews were busy inflating balloons for the next event. Even muted by the haze, the colors gleamed in the late-afternoon light. Frank wished he could just relax and enjoy the event as an ordinary spectator. But he knew he wouldn't want to give up the thrill of carrying out an important investigation that could save the IBC a whole lot of money and trouble—not to mention save some people's lives.

Marie Thibault was standing on the front porch of the hotel, passing out envelopes to a small crowd of balloonists.

"Those must be the FIFO maps," Alicia said. "Here, I'll show you how it works." She went up and spoke to Thibault, who handed her an envelope.

"See?" Alicia said, pulling a photocopied map from the envelope. "That *X* marks the first target. If I think I'll do best going east from there, I choose a target in that direction and mark it. Got it?"

"Yep," Frank said, taking the map she gave him. Alicia went inside to look for her father.

Frank watched her go, then glanced at the map in his hand. After a closer look, he smiled.

"Joe?" he said. "You remember that time Dad took us camping on the Ten Broeck River?"

Joe laughed. "Do I. We brought the tent and everything, about five miles in from the road. It was going to be a real wilderness experience. I'll never forget Dad's face when he realized our campsite was right under a high-voltage power line."

"Remember the way the wires hummed all night?" Frank said. "Well, look at this. There it is, the Ten Broeck River. It's not that far from here." He pointed to the *X* that marked the first target, right by the river.

"I wonder if we can find that campsite again," Joe said.

"That should be easy. Just follow the power line," Frank said. "Let's see, now . . . That's funny. It's not marked."

"A power line? It should be," Chet said, peeking over Frank's shoulder. "Don't all these topographical maps show high-tension lines?"

"Not this one," Frank said. When he realized what this meant, his breath caught in his throat. "That *X* must be right next to the power line. And most of the balloons in the meet are headed straight for it. If it's not on their maps and they can't spot the cables in this haze . . ."

The rest was obvious. The wires carried hundreds of volts. If a balloon got snagged on one of them, the pilot could easily be electrocuted.

Frank looked around. A rainbow-colored balloon was just rising from the field and starting to move eastward. He could just make out another balloon, about to disappear over the treetops and into the haze. Most of the rest of the pack were already well on their way to the target.

"We've got to warn everybody," Frank said. "Quick. Before it's too late."

Chapter 11

"CHET, JOE, GET DOWN to the field right away," Frank said. "Warn everybody. See if you can stop any of them from taking off. I'll go find Elwell."

Joe and Chet sprinted across the lawn toward the meadow. Frank dashed up the steps to the hotel and burst through the open door of the IBC office. Marie Thibault and two of the staffers looked up, startled.

"Where's Fred Elwell?" Frank demanded. "We've got an emergency."

"He's in a meeting," Thibault said. "The Wapiti Room, down at the end of the hall. What—"

Frank was out the door and down the hall in a flash, carrying the map in his right hand.

The door to the Wapiti Room was ajar. Frank barged in. Elwell and half a dozen others were sitting around a table. Alicia was standing near the window. Everybody looked surprised.

"The FIFO target," Frank said, catching his breath. "It's right next to a power line that's not marked on the map. You've got to stop the event."

"Let me see that," a woman with a blond ponytail and a square chin said. She grabbed the map from Frank's hand, scanned it quickly, then said, "Fred, he's right. That isn't the target we chose. It's not even the same map."

Elwell sprang to his feet and came over to take a quick look.

"Chet and Joe went to the field to warn everybody," Frank said. "A lot of the balloons were already launched. Can you contact them by radio?"

"We can try," Elwell replied. "But not everybody carries a radio, and some of them don't bother to monitor it if they do." He looked around the table. "Dave?" he said to Alicia's father. "My car's right out front. Use my radio. See if you can raise anybody who already took off. Who's got a list of entries?"

Several people started checking their bags and jacket pockets. A tall man with a cowboy hat found his list first and handed it to Elwell, saying, "There you go, Fred."

"This says who's in the FIFO, their call signs and radio frequencies," Elwell said, handing the list to Dave Davidson.

"Roger," Davidson said, beckoning for his daughter to follow.

Alicia hurried across the room. As she passed Frank, she said, "Why don't you come with us?"

The three ran down the hallway and out the front door. The blue all-wheel-drive wagon was the same one Frank had ridden in right after Joe's midair leap. Had it really been only the day before?

Alicia's dad jumped into the front seat, started the wagon, and grabbed the handset of the two-way radio. Alicia climbed into the front passenger seat, while Frank jerked open the rear door and piled in. It took them almost fifteen minutes to contact eight of the eleven competitors who had already taken off. That left three. Depending on wind conditions, they could be on top of the power lines by now.

"We're just going to have to chase them and try to signal," Dave Davidson said. "Frank, you've got the map?"

Frank said, "Yes sir."

"Good," Alicia's dad said. "You navigate. Alicia, you keep a close watch on the sky. We know where they're headed. Let's just hope we can get a jump on them."

As they drove toward the exit, Frank studied the photocopied map for a route that would bring them close to the marked target. There wasn't one. The nearest paved road was at least a couple of miles away. He remembered that from their camping trip.

There had to be an access road for the work crews who maintained the power line, he thought, but he didn't see one marked on the map. That was no surprise. The power line wasn't marked, so why would the access road be?

"Take a left at the main road," Frank said, going with his best hunch. "Go right three miles farther on Battenburg Pike." He was estimating where it was that the power lines crossed the road.

After about four miles, Frank said, "The lines should cross the road about a mile up ahead." Sure enough, they did. "Slow down," Frank said. "This is where we go cross-country."

The access road was really just a trail at the base of the pylons. Alicia's dad put the transmission in low and eased off the road. He tried to keep up a reasonable speed and steer around the worst of the bumps, but even so, Frank's head bounced off the ceiling a few times. They crested a small ridge and started heading down toward the river.

"Whoa," Dave Davidson said. "There's our first one." Half a mile or more up ahead, a large white balloon with red vertical stripes was emerging from the haze. It had come up over the ridge and was maybe fifteen feet above the treetops now, drifting right down toward one of the pylons that held up the power lines.

Dave Davidson gave five or six long blasts of the horn, but they had no way of knowing whether the balloonist heard. They kept charging forward over the rough terrain, beeping the horn all the way.

Had the balloonist seen the power lines yet? Had he or she heard their warning? One minute Frank couldn't tell, the next minute he could see the helmeted figure suddenly scramble to ignite the balloon's burner. The pilot leaned helplessly over the edge of the basket and peered down at the pylon, which Frank figured must be at least eighty-five feet tall, waiting for the balloon to start its ascent. Seconds later it floated clear of the wires by less than ten feet.

"That's one close call," Dave Davidson said, pulling to a stop in a wide clearing just short of where the balloon had cleared the pylon. "This must be the landing site. The question is, where are the rest of them, and how do we signal them?" He picked up the radio handset and tried again to contact the two balloons that were still out there. No answer.

Meanwhile Frank rummaged around the inside of the wagon. He was hoping to find a spotlight, a smoke bomb, or a flare gun, but the IBC wagon was altogether too tidy for his purposes.

"Dad," Alicia said, pointing back and to their right. "I just caught sight of another one through the trees. About three hundred yards and closing fast."

Frank quickly craned his neck and peered out his window. He couldn't see the second balloon. But he did realize that the ground on their left sloped steeply down to the river.

"I've got an idea," he said. "Mr. Davidson, if you back the car downhill, you can aim the headlights up. We'll flash 'em *and* beep 'em."

Dave Davidson slipped the wagon into reverse and carefully edged it far enough down the slope so that its hood was pointed up at nearly a forty-five degree angle. He pulled back on the high-beam flasher with his left hand while he hit the horn repeatedly with his right.

The big purple-and-gold globe floated into sight just above the treetops. The balloon was less than fifty yards from the power lines and still coming. Visibility was patchy, but the balloonist had to see them or hear them. Would he or she understand the warning? At last they saw the burner come to life. As the balloon began to rise out of danger, its pilot leaned out of the basket to wave thanks.

They waited for the third balloon, which arrived about five minutes later from roughly the same direction. This time, the honking and flashing worked like a charm.

"Well, that's three out of three," Dave Davidson said. "Let's head back and let everybody know."

They were quiet as Mr. Davidson negotiated the track under the pylons back to the main road. Once they were cruising smoothly on pavement again, Alicia said, "I wonder what happened with those maps. How do you think they managed to hand out a completely different one from the one they were supposed to?"

Frank wondered, too. He knew they couldn't afford to let up until they found out who was responsible. The acts of sabotage were coming faster. At first only the top competitors and rivals had been targeted, one by one—Dutch Festinger, Paco Amaya, Mark Svoboda, and of course Alicia. Then the Hardys themselves had become possible targets. Now an entire event had been sabotaged.

Who was it? An insider? It was clearly

somebody who knew enough about ballooning and about how these events were set up to cause some pretty serious damage. Maybe the maps would provide enough evidence to lead them to the culprit.

Joe and Chet were waiting on the veranda of the hotel when Frank pulled up with the Davidsons in the IBC's blue wagon.

Frank jumped out and took the steps two at a time. "Any idea how that map got passed out?" he asked Joe.

Joe shook his head. "Elwell wanted to question the office staff himself, but we talked him into waiting until you got back."

The three went inside and tapped on the office door. Elwell opened it. When he saw them, he stepped outside and closed the door behind him. Joe noticed that the lines on his face had deepened.

"I've got some information," he said. "Our FIFO committee chose the first target shortly after lunch. It was marked on a map, put in a folder, and left in the office for reproduction."

"When was this?" Joe asked.

"Just after two," Elwell replied. "Zoë, one of our staff, made copies of the map and put them in envelopes for distribution. That was between three-fifteen and three-thirty. But the map she copied was not the one the committee had left. The target was moved, and the power line was whited out."

"Who could have switched the maps?" Chet asked.

"Anyone," Elwell said. "The place was wide open. At least one of the staff was always in the room, but they were busy."

"We'd better talk to them," Frank said.

"Go right ahead," Elwell said.

Elwell led them inside. Marie Thibault was standing next to one of the desks. There was a dark-haired girl at the desk, wiping away tears. From the adjoining desk, a guy with shaggy hair and a faint mustache was watching sympathetically.

Elwell cleared his throat. He introduced the Hardys and said, "I know you folks won't mind answering a few questions. Frank, Joe?"

After exchanging a glance with Frank, Joe asked, "Where was the folder with the map in it?"

"In the basket next to the copier," Thibault said.

"Did anyone notice anybody messing with it?" Joe asked.

Thibault chuckled. "We were so busy, I wouldn't have noticed if a herd of elephants came through here!"

"How about you guys?" Frank asked the other two staffers. They shook their heads.

"Which of you did the copying? Where was the folder in the basket? Was it marked?"

The girl who'd been crying raised her hand. "It was right on top," she said. "And there was a note on it that said something like, 'FIFO Map—thirty copies by four o'clock.' I didn't even look at the map. I just made the copies and put them in envelopes. It's not my fault. Really it isn't."

"We know that, Zoë," Elwell said. "Don't worry about it." He turned to Chet and the Hardys and said in a low voice, "How about you talk to her later, after she calms down?"

"Okay," Frank said. "Is Max Arneson around?"

"He had meetings most of the day," Elwell replied. "He should be back soon."

"Can we get together with you two in about fifteen minutes?" Frank asked.

"Certainly," Elwell replied. "I'll ask him to join us as soon as he gets here."

Frank led Joe and Chet outside onto the lawn. They huddled out of anyone's hearing range. "So what do we do now?" Chet asked.

"Wait for the extortionist to demand the money," Frank said. "Make sure we have a plan for when he does, and follow up on our leads in the meantime."

"We've either got to pay up and set a trap or stall him long enough to catch him," Joe said.

"I'd say stall," Frank said. "But this guy seems to have good inside information. Look how he switched the maps right under everybody's noses. That was pretty slick. If he found out we were stalling, he might stage another accident just to punish us."

"So we do a fake payoff," Joe said. "Go along with his plan, stake out the payoff site, drop off a package of phony money, then catch him in the act picking it up?"

Chet saw Arneson go inside and suggested they follow him. Inside, the Lift executive had just met Fred Elwell in the lobby. Elwell beckoned Chet and the Hardys over, then with a brief word led the group down the hall to a small conference room with a table in the center.

They were all taking their places at the table when Frank caught a glimpse of movement out of the corner of his eye. He turned to get a better look, but before he had a chance to focus, there was a loud crash, and one of the windowpanes exploded into a million tiny pieces, showering slivers of glass all over the conference room.

Chapter 12

JOE WAS CLOSEST to the window. At the sound of the crash, he instinctively covered his face with his arms. Something hit the floor with a thud and rolled over his foot. "Get back!" he shouted, jumping away. Then he turned and saw that it wasn't a bomb—it was only half a brick with an envelope taped to it.

Joe bent down to look at the envelope. It was addressed to "The Hardys." The typeface appeared to be the same as the previous notes—fourteen-point Helvetica.

Frank knelt down next to Joe and took the envelope off the brick. He opened it and read it aloud.

" 'Okay, Snoops, here are your instructions.

Send the $100,000 by balloon, tomorrow at eight a.m. over Pioneer Park. Drop it on the red *X*. Don't miss, or the Lift Challenge will become your worst nightmare.' "

The only sound in the room was the crunch of glass fragments as they all brushed themselves off, straightened up, and started to take their seats again.

"We were expecting something like this," Chet finally said.

"And we think we have a plan," Frank said, and went on to expand on Joe's idea for Elwell and Arneson. They would send one of the balloons over to Pioneer Park to drop a packet of dummy bills on the marked spot. Frank, Joe, and Chet would chase the balloon in a four-wheel-drive vehicle, staying in radio contact on a frequency not normally used by balloonists. After the pickup, they'd follow the extortionist from the drop site and either make the arrest themselves or call for backup.

Elwell agreed to the plan. Arneson went along with it, although he was a little less enthusiastic.

"It's a risky strategy," the Lift executive said. "But I guess as long as you don't lose the guy's trail, we'll be all right."

A quick check of the list of entries for the Lift Challenge revealed that Dave Davidson was not competing. They contacted him, and he said he'd be more than happy to help out by dropping the packet at Pioneer Park. They agreed to use a radio frequency that was normally reserved for private planes flying out of Bayport Airport. Frank called the airport and got permission to use it from his contacts there.

That evening at dinner, the Hardys and Chet sat with Alicia and Dave Davidson. They were just settling down to eat when there was a murmur on the other side of the room. Most of the diners turned to look out the big windows over by the kitchen side of the dining hall.

An armored car had just pulled up to the delivery entrance, and it was visible from the corner of the hall. One guard got out and stood watch. Two other uniformed men took a cloth-wrapped package from the back of the truck and carried it into the hotel.

Alicia stood up to get a better view. "That must be the prize money for the Lift Challenge," she said. "It's going to be pretty exciting to see the winner get all that cash, right in front of a big crowd, with all the television cameras and everything."

"And all the tax officials taking careful notes," her father said wryly. "Are you sorry I didn't enter?"

"Of course not," said Alicia, who had volunteered to go with her dad on the Pioneer Park drop the next day. She turned to the Hardys and explained that her father was developing high blood pressure and his doctor had recommended that he avoid any unnecessary stress. "So he kept right on ballooning," she said, "but he pulled out of competition."

Her father smiled. "You fellows may not believe it after what you've seen the last couple of days," he said, "but this sport is usually very relaxing. Once you get up there, it's almost like meditation."

Frank couldn't argue with that statement. He recalled the feeling of timelessness and tranquility he had during the flight with Mark Svoboda—before they discovered the problem with the compass. He wanted to try another balloon flight sometime, with no sabotage.

They were finishing dessert when Joe looked up and saw Paco Amaya crossing the room, headed straight for their table. He was dressed up, wearing a dark blue satin Western shirt and a bolo tie with a silver-and-turquoise thunderbird clasp. His black hair was slicked back and gleaming under the light of the rustic chandeliers.

Joe eased his chair back from the table, giving himself a little extra room to move, in case he suddenly needed it.

"Evening, all," Amaya said with a nod and

a serious expression on his face. "Joe, could I have a word with you outside?"

"Paco, enough is enough, all right?" Dave Davidson said.

"I mean a *peaceful* word," Amaya said with a hint of a smile.

Joe stood up. "All right," he said. He followed Amaya toward the door, relaxing a bit but not letting down his guard entirely.

In the hallway, Amaya faced him and said, "This afternoon I made a fool of myself. I wanted to say I'm sorry."

"Okay, sure," Joe said. Amaya extended his hand, and Joe, still a little wary, shook it.

"It's no excuse," Amaya continued, "but I've had a lot on my mind lately. I work at an Air Force base that's closing down, so I'm out of a job. I wanted to start my own balloon charter outfit, but that takes money. When it looked like that dirty trick might get me disqualified from the Lift Challenge tomorrow, I really lost it."

"I can understand that," Joe said. "But why pick on us?"

"There was all this trouble, and nobody was questioning what you two were doing here," Amaya said. "I guess I thought you were ruining our cozy little sport. Balloonists are a pretty tight group, even though we're competitive. So I guess I just blamed the outsiders.

When Fred Elwell vouched for you, that started me thinking. I've got to respect his opinion."

Joe nodded. "I'm glad you changed your mind about us," he said. "But don't forget—*somebody* put that noose in your camper and took that magnet. If I were you, I'd start locking my door."

"Thanks," Amaya replied. "I'll think about it." Joe knew that much was true. He'd think about it. But the real question was, would he do anything about it?

Later that evening Chet, Frank, and Joe met privately with Elwell, Arneson, Dave Davidson, and Alicia to review their plans for the dropoff.

After the meeting Alicia said to Frank, "So, you guys are detectives. I *knew* there was something you weren't telling me. Why all the secrecy? Am I a suspect or something?"

"Normally, we don't like to tip our hand to the crooks," Frank said. "You'd be surprised how many of them make dumb mistakes when they don't realize that someone's after them. After this latest note, though, it's obvious that the extortionist knows who we are. So it's not such a big secret anymore."

He smiled and added, "Anyway, by tomorrow morning, you'd have worked it out for yourself."

* * *

The next morning the sun rose in a cloudless sky. It was a perfect day for the Lift Challenge.

Chet, Joe, and Frank had left the hotel just before sunrise in Fred Elwell's 4x4 wagon. Now they were parked in a roadside rest area near the main entrance to Pioneer State Park.

"I can't believe we had to leave before six if the drop isn't until eight," Chet grumbled. "We all could have had an extra hour's sleep."

"The whole idea was to sneak out here before anybody could see us," Joe replied. "Here, I talked one of the waiters into slipping me some of these." Joe handed Chet a bundle of fresh cinnamon buns wrapped in a napkin.

"Thanks, Joe," Chet said, then hastily added, "Just kidding, Joe. I'll pass them around."

Frank, who was at the wheel, said, "Pipe down, guys." There was a burst of static from the two-way radio. Frank turned up the volume, and Dave Davidson's voice came through loud and clear. "Seven Niner Zero Chase," he said. "This is Balloon Seven Niner Zero preparing for takeoff. Acknowledge. Over."

Frank thumbed the talk button and said, "Roger, Balloon Seven Niner Zero. We hear you loud and clear. Over."

There was a long pause. Then they heard Dave Davidson say, "Seven Niner Zero Chase,

I'm aloft. My heading is one hundred twenty-five-degrees, speed fifteen knots, ETA over target oh-eight-oh-five local."

"Did you hear that, Chet?" Joe whispered. "They'll be over the park in about ten minutes."

Joe unfolded the large-scale topographical map and spread it across his knees. Pioneer had recently been added to the state park system and was still undeveloped. A single paved road led to the old mansion that served as park headquarters. The rest of the big, thickly wooded tract was accessible only by old lumber roads and fire trails.

"How do Alicia and her dad know where to drop the package?" Chet asked.

"We'll have to wait and see," Frank replied. "They usually mark targets with a big *X* made from strips of cloth."

Alicia's voice came over the radio. "We see the target," she said in a steady voice. "It's in a big clearing. The coordinates are—hold on—two-six minutes three-eight seconds north, zero-eight minutes one-seven seconds west. We'll try to hold up the drop until you're in position."

While she repeated the numbers, Frank started the engine.

Joe hastily traced the grid markings with his index finger. "Got it," he said. "A little over a mile up the access road, there's a Jeep trail off to the right. Let's roll."

It was Chet who spotted the entrance to the overgrown track. Tree branches scraped along both sides of the wagon. It sounded like fingernails on a blackboard. Frank winced; he hated that sound. There was scrub brush growing on the middle of the track, some of it almost waist-high. It didn't look as if any vehicle had been this way in years.

"Can we make it?" Chet asked anxiously.

"We have to," Frank replied as he shifted the transmission into low gear. "Joe, how much farther to that clearing?"

"A couple of hundred yards," Joe replied. "But I just noticed this little blue line on the map between here and there. I think there's a—"

"I can see it," Frank said, hitting the brakes. Just beyond a stand of trees, the track dipped down the bank of a narrow stream and reappeared on the other side of the water. "Okay, out, quick. I'm going to go for it. Be ready to push on the other side."

Joe and Chet jumped out and stood well off the trail. Frank backed up a few yards to get a running start. He gave it some gas, and the rear end of the 4x4 fishtailed as it sped down the slippery bank. Joe and Chet ran after it into the stream. The water was barely knee-deep but icy cold.

"Get ready," Joe shouted. The wagon slowed almost to a stop as it reached the far side of the stream bed. Joe put his shoulder to the tailgate and dug his feet in. The engine roared. The wheels started to spin, sending up a spray of water and gravel. Joe turned his face away and shoved harder.

Suddenly, the wagon zipped up the bank. He and Chet went sprawling in the mud.

They scrambled up the bank and jumped in. "Very funny," Chet muttered as Frank hit the accelerator. "Too bad nobody caught it on home video."

"Seven Niner Zero Chase, we are now making the drop." Dave Davidson's voice came over the radio. Frank quickly reached out and turned down the volume. "Good luck. Over and out."

Joe slapped the dashboard in frustration. He could just see a bright patch through the trees that marked the clearing. The extortionist was probably collecting the package right at this moment. They were still chugging along the old trail, and the guy would probably be gone by the time they made it to the clearing.

Just as they burst out of the woods into a big field of tall grass, Joe heard the ripping sound of a motorcycle engine winding up to high revs.

"There!" Chet said, pointing off to the right. "He went down that road!"

Frank spun the wheel, putting the van into a four-wheel drift on the grass. The "road" Chet saw was a fire lane even narrower and more overgrown than the one they had just followed.

There was a curve after the road left the clearing, and Frank took it as fast as possible. They bounced wildly over the ruts as Frank picked up speed on the next straightaway. Suddenly, they rounded another curve, and Frank slammed on the brakes, fighting to keep the 4x4 from skidding off into the woods. A big pine tree, probably blown down by a winter storm, was completely blocking their path. Broken underbrush showed where the motorcycle had circled around the ball of roots, but there was no room for the van to pass.

Joe stared down at the map. "Frank, this trail circles back to the clearing," he said. "If you can back up quick enough, you'll catch him."

"No way," Frank replied. "This track's too narrow. I can't make any speed going backward."

Joe yanked at the door handle, shoved the door open with his shoulder, and hit the ground running. How far back was the clearing—a hundred yards or so? He'd sprinted that distance lots of times, but not usually trying to catch a motorcycle.

Just inside the clearing, Joe stopped and stood, catching his breath. There was no sign of the extortionist. Had he already passed through? Or maybe found a different escape route?

Suddenly, from somewhere very close by, Joe could hear the high-pitched whine of a two-cycle engine straining at maximum revs.

Joe ran in the direction of the sound. He was nearing the edge of the clearing when the motorcycle burst into view. Its rider was crouching low over the handlebars. He must have seen Joe right about the same time Joe saw him. With a staccato roar, the bike swerved and headed straight at Joe.

Chapter 13

JOE CHARGED STRAIGHT at the motorcyclist and let out a blood-curdling yell. The bike kept speeding straight at him.

Joe tensed himself, ready to dive out of the way. But the rider lost his nerve first and swung wildly to the left. The motorcycle's tires skidded on the grass, then bit in, splattering dirt and pebbles. Joe turned his head to dodge the worst of it. When he looked back, the bike was already into the woods.

The blue 4x4 backed into the clearing. Frank and Chet jumped out and ran over.

"He got away?" Chet asked.

"Afraid so," Joe said.

"He's going to be pretty ticked off when he

unwraps that package and finds a big bundle of waste paper instead of the hundred thousand dollars," Frank said. "Did you get a look at him, at least?"

"Not his face," Joe said. "He was wearing a visor. But he was dressed in black—and riding a purple motorcycle."

There was a short silence while Frank and Chet took in this information. Then Frank said, "A purple motorcycle? Paco Amaya?"

"It fit the description of Paco's bike."

"It's hard to believe it was Paco," Frank said.

"Especially after the way he apologized to me last night," Joe said.

"The crook must have used Paco's bike as part of the frame he's been trying to hang on Paco all along," Frank said.

Joe recalled his conversation with Amaya. "He told me he was out of a job. That could be a first-class motive."

"But why would he have told you that if he was the extortionist?" Frank demanded. "It doesn't make sense."

"How about this?" Joe said. "Paco's been framing himself but doing it so obviously that everyone will think he's being framed and that means he must be innocent."

"That's right," Chet said. "What's that saying about the spy business being a hall of mirrors?"

"Hold on," Frank said. "There is such a thing as being too clever and getting caught in your own trap. Why don't we just head back to the Wilderland, before whoever's doing this has time to react to the phony money?"

"Wait. Maybe we can find a decent tire print from that bike," Joe said. "I'd like to know for sure if it was Paco's."

They fanned out and scoured the area. After a couple of minutes, Chet found a patch of soft dirt. "There's a nice one right here," he said.

Frank and Joe joined him. The tire print was very clear. Frank pulled out a small notebook he kept in his back pocket and made a quick but accurate sketch of it. Then they all piled into the 4x4 for the trip back to the Wilderland.

It was the biggest day of the International Balloonfest, the grand finale, and the crowds were already gathering. The guard at the gate saw the official sticker on the windshield of Elwell's car and waved them through. Frank parked in front of the hotel, and the three teens hurried around to the side lot. Frank was half expecting to see an empty space where Amaya's camper had been parked. But the camper was still there. So was the purple motorcycle.

Joe went over to it and gingerly touched the cooling fins of the motor. "Still warm," he reported. "And the key's in the ignition. The guy never learns, does he?"

Chet knocked on the door of the camper, and there was no answer. Then he tried the handle. No luck. "At least he locked this," he said.

Frank took out his tire-tread sketch and checked it against the tire. One glance was enough. It was a perfect match.

Frank stood up, stretched, and gazed around the parking lot. Where was the rider? And *who* was it? He started reviewing the facts of the case, and after a few moments, he found himself staring at a wire litter basket on the walk next to the side entrance of the hotel. The hotel staff didn't seem to empty it very often. It was almost overflowing with newspapers, potato chip bags, soda cans, and other trash. He kept staring. There was something familiar in there, but he couldn't quite place it. He walked over to take a closer look. It was the package! He reached in and dug it out.

"What is it?" Chet asked.

Frank turned and showed Chet and Joe the

open cloth wrapper with scrap paper tumbling out of it.

"The fake extortion money," he said. "The bike rider must have waited to get back here to look inside the package, then chucked it right away. We'd better get down to the field. If he's going to pull anything, that's where it'll happen."

The Hardys and Chet edged through the crowds of spectators to the fence surrounding the field and showed their passes at the gate. Just as they went in, there was a loud cheer from the crowd. Frank looked up. The big balloon shaped like a bottle of Lift had just left the ground and was floating over the field, heading eastward.

"Where's Paco?" Joe said, scanning the rows of balloons for a red-white-and-green one.

"He probably hasn't started inflating yet," Chet said. "Let's try the far end of the lefthand row. That's where he was yesterday."

As they headed down the rows of balloons, Joe spotted Amaya. He was standing inside his basket, reaching over his head to work on the burner. The balloon envelope was lying nearby, still folded up.

"Hey, fellas," he said in a cautious tone as they approached. "What's happening?"

"Nothing much. Getting ready for the big event?" Joe replied.

Amaya nodded. "You bet. I've been out here since before breakfast, checking over every inch of my rig. My gut feeling is that winning the Challenge is going to come down to the last quarter mile. So every single detail matters."

Frank glanced around. "No motorcycle?" he asked.

"I can still manage to walk this far," Amaya replied sardonically. "Why, do you want to borrow it? Everybody else just takes it without asking."

"How do you mean?" Chet asked.

"I took a coffee break this morning, and I actually saw somebody riding off on my bike," Amaya said. "Would you believe it? He didn't even bother to wave."

"Who was it?" Frank asked.

"I wish I knew," Amaya replied. "I'd like to teach him some manners." He leaned over to rummage through a tool box. When he straightened up, he said, "Okay. Unless you guys have anything else, I'm just going to get back to work here."

"Nothing else right now," Joe said.

"Hey, good luck this afternoon," Chet said.

As they walked away, Frank noticed a young woman in a green jumpsuit working on the balloon next to Amaya's. He went over to her and said, "Sorry to bother you, but could you help me settle a bet? My friend Chet swears he came looking for Paco Amaya earlier and couldn't find him. I say Chet must have looked in the wrong spot, because Paco told me he was here all morning."

"You win," the woman said. "I've been here since around eight, and Paco's been working on his balloon the whole time."

Frank thanked her and rejoined his friends. "Paco's got an alibi for this morning," he said.

"Unless he's working with an accomplice," Joe said.

"Right," Chet said. "So where does that leave us?"

"With Harris Scott," Joe said. "Let's go see if he's in."

They walked over to the *Earthquest* capsule. A TV camera crew was just leaving the exhibit. The reporter looked angry. Frank heard him mutter as he walked away: "I'll remember to stand him up the next time he makes an appointment with me."

They saw a hand-lettered sign that said "Closed till 1:00" taped to the door of the capsule.

"It must be something awfully important to make him skip a TV interview and close his exhibit right in the middle of the big day," Joe said.

"Let's check the hotel," Chet suggested.

They went over to the hotel and walked straight to the front desk. Frank asked if Mr. Scott was in. The clerk glanced over his shoulder at the mailboxes. "Mr. Scott's key is there," he said. "And there have been several messages for him this morning that he hasn't picked up. He must have gone out. Would you like to leave a note?"

"No, thanks," Frank said. "This looks like a dead end," he said under his breath to Joe and Chet. "Let's go back to *Earthquest.* Maybe someone around there has seen him."

As they turned away from the desk, Frank saw Fred Elwell hurrying across the lobby toward them. "I've been looking all over for you," he said. "I knew you were back because I saw my car out front. I tuned in on the drop, but what happened after that?"

Frank glanced around the crowded lobby. "Let's go talk in private," he said. "Is there anyone in the office?"

"I doubt it," Elwell replied. "Let's go."

The door to the office was ajar. Elwell stopped and said, "That's odd," with a puzzled expression.

Frank felt his stomach sink. "Excuse me," he said, and pushed past Elwell into the office. Joe and Chet were close behind him, followed by Elwell.

"What is it?" the IBC president asked.

Frank hurried across the room to the big old-fashioned safe and grabbed its shiny handle. It turned with a click, and the heavy steel door swung open.

Frank took one look inside, then turned to Elwell. "The safe was unlocked," he said. "And the money—it's gone!"

Chapter 14

"IMPOSSIBLE!" ELWELL EXCLAIMED. He hurried over to Frank's side and peered into the safe. After a moment of stunned silence, he said slowly, "This is a catastrophe."

"What's the matter?" somebody said from the doorway. Frank looked over his shoulder. Marie Thibault was standing there. She looked pale.

"Marie, did you leave the safe open?" Elwell asked.

"Me? Of course not," she replied. "I just came downstairs a little while ago. My alarm didn't go off this morning. I overslept. What's wrong—is something missing?"

"You'd better believe it," Joe said. "The Lift Challenge prize money is gone."

"Oh." Thibault's eyes widened. "It must have been that guy in black who took it."

"What guy?" Frank demanded. "When?"

"A few minutes ago," she told him. "I was leaving the dining room when I saw somebody in a black motorcycle helmet coming from this direction. He had a backpack over one arm."

"Which way did he go?" Joe asked.

"Down the hall, toward the side door," she said.

"Let's fan out and get him," Joe said to Frank and Chet. "I'll check Paco's camper. You guys go to the main gate and the field. Somebody must have seen him."

Ten minutes later Chet and the two Hardys met back in the lobby, out of breath and empty-handed. "Nobody saw anything," Frank reported.

"Same here," Joe said.

"Ditto," Chet said.

They went back to the office. Fred Elwell and Marie Thibault were facing each other across his desk, looking glum.

"I just got off the phone with the state police," Elwell said. "They're sending some troopers over. So's the local sheriff's department. But we've got at least ten thousand spectators out there. They can't search everybody."

"Mr. Elwell?" Chet said. "Is there any way

someone could have gotten the combination to the safe?"

Elwell's face reddened. "Well . . ." he said.

"We've only been using this office for a week, not long enough to memorize the combination," Marie Thibault said stiffly. "And there's stuff in the safe that we need to get to all the time."

Frank let out a groan. "Let me guess," he said. "You keep the combination on an index card in your desk drawer."

Her cheeks turned pink. "Well, no," she said. "It's in the address file. Under *C.*"

Joe shook his head in disbelief. "Anybody who's spent any time in the office could have seen you looking it up," he said.

"You don't expect the people you work with to be thieves," she retorted.

Frank turned to Elwell. "We're going to have to tell Max Arneson," he said. Elwell said he'd already called Arneson out of a meeting and asked him to come to the office. After a few minutes of awkward silence, they could all hear someone hurrying down the hall.

"All right, what is it now?" Arneson demanded as he burst into the office.

Elwell went over and spoke to him in a low voice. The conversation was punctuated by several groans from Arneson. When Elwell finished, Arneson said, "I know this isn't your fault, Fred, but do me a favor. Don't come to me with any more projects."

"Come on," Frank said softly to Chet and Joe. "Let's see if we can track down Harris Scott."

"Did you say Harris?" Arneson said. "Harris Scott? There's no way he's mixed up in any of this."

"No," Frank said hastily. "We thought there might have been somebody snooping around his exhibit earlier, and we wanted to ask him about it. He hasn't been around all morning."

"Of course he has," Arneson replied. "He's been in a meeting with me. We had some business matters to discuss."

"This morning?" Joe asked.

"Yes, this morning," Arneson told him. "And yesterday afternoon as well. Do you have a problem with that?"

Joe just shook his head.

"Max, we'd better talk about how you'd like to handle this," Elwell said to Arneson, who nodded grimly.

"If you gentlemen will excuse us," Frank said. "We need to—"

"Just go," Arneson said. "And this time, if you catch the guy, don't let him get away."

The Hardys and Chet left the IBC office, went out to the veranda, and pulled three chairs into a circle.

"There went our best suspect," Joe said.

"Let's face it," Chet added, "it could be anybody with access. It could even be Elwell or Arneson or Thibault. We've got plenty of suspects; we just don't have any clues."

"Not true," Frank interjected. "We've got plenty of clues. We just haven't made sense of them yet. *Somebody* sabotaged Dutch Festinger's balloon and put the magnet on Mark Svoboda's compass and slashed Alicia Davidson's deflation cord. *Somebody* sent those extortion notes. And there was *somebody* on that bike we chased through the woods this morning."

Joe rubbed his chin. "You know, when I'm doing a jigsaw puzzle, I like to start in one corner and try to put that together, then move on to another part. Maybe we can do the same thing here. Why don't we focus on just one part of the case? Let's say the sabotage, since that came first. What's the motive?"

"Extortion, obviously," Chet said.

"Sure, but forget about the extortion for a minute," Joe said. "Let's just focus on the sabotage."

"Somebody is trying to eliminate his rivals and win the Lift Challenge," Frank said. "That just brings us back to square one, to the top three—Festinger, Amaya, and Svoboda."

"What about opportunity?" Joe asked.

"Anybody could have fiddled with Festinger's balloon," Chet said. "But what about putting the magnet on Svoboda's compass? What was it they said?"

"According to Sue and Ron on his ground crew," Frank said, "they had the balloon in sight from the preflight check until takeoff. Then Svoboda admitted he left the balloon for a few minutes. And he said Paco Amaya was nearby."

"Which puts Paco back in the running," Chet said. "That leaves Alicia's deflation cord. Somebody slashed it when she and I went over to see what all the ruckus was between you guys and Paco."

"We had Festinger and Amaya right under our noses that whole time," Frank said slowly. "But Mark Svoboda wasn't there. Remember, Joe? I yelled for him, and there wasn't any answer."

"We eliminated him as a suspect because we figured he couldn't have written the extortion notes since he was never in the office," Joe said. "But what if—"

"Are you saying that he messed up his own compass so he'd look like a victim?" Chet said. "That's taking a pretty big risk."

Joe's jaw dropped. "I just thought of something," he said. "That watch he was wearing has a built-in altimeter, a barometer, half a dozen other functions, and a compass. He could have faked the whole lost-at-sea bit."

"Let's go find him before he takes off," Frank said. "If he faked that whole thing, he could be our man."

Frank scanned the dozens of balloons on the field and quickly spotted the one with the blue and white checkerboard pattern. "There," he said. "We'd better hurry. He's just about ready to go."

As they headed toward Svoboda's rig, they heard Fred Elwell's voice blaring over the public address system. He welcomed everyone and thanked Lift soda for sponsoring the meet, then said, "In a few minutes, the first contestants in the Lift Challenge will take to the sky. They're going to be competing for a prize of one hundred thousand dollars in cash."

With that statement, he had the attention of just about everyone in the crowd.

"For those of you who are new to this event," Elwell continued, "here's how it works. Each contestant receives a standard propane tank with ten gallons of fuel. For an average hot-air balloon, the type called an AX-Seven, that's enough to stay aloft for about an hour. The balloonist who manages to go the greatest distance on his or her fuel is our winner.

"In case you were wondering, we have winds of about twenty-five miles an hour up there, so if we allow a few minutes at each end of the flight for ascent and descent, we can expect our winner to go about eighteen to twenty miles."

Frank, Joe, and Chet made their way quickly through the crowds. Once inside the enclosure, they broke into a run. There were already half a dozen balloons in the air, moving eastward. Frank kept his eyes fixed on Mark Svoboda's balloon. Was it starting to rise?

Frank could see Svoboda standing in the basket, talking to his ground crew. Only twenty or thirty yards to go. Svoboda glanced around, and his eyes met Frank's. A frown crossed his face, and he spat out a few words at his two crew members. Then he quickly reached for the burner lanyard.

A six-foot-long flame of blue and orange leaped upward into the mouth of the balloon. After a second or two, the balloon began to rise. It was only a few inches off the ground, then a foot, two feet . . .

Frank was sprinting now. He put everything he had into a last burst of speed and a powerful leap. His hands slapped down on the padded rim of the basket, and his fingers closed tightly around it.

The balloon dipped under Frank's weight, and his feet touched the ground momentarily. He pushed off immediately and managed to hook his arms over the edge of the basket. Then he pivoted at the waist, hoping to get one foot up over the rim. This shouldn't be much harder than shinnying over a fence, he thought.

Suddenly, he felt Svoboda grab his right arm at the wrist and lever it upward. As he fought back, Frank glanced back over his shoulder.

The balloon was already more than one hundred feet in the air, and Frank was losing his grip. He realized that he couldn't hang on much longer.

Chapter 15

FRANK FELT DROPS of sweat pop out on his forehead. He was putting almost every ounce of his strength into keeping his grip on the balloon basket. He felt Svoboda give another tug at his arm. Luckily, Svoboda couldn't use both hands because he was busy with one of them holding down the burner lanyard so the balloon would keep rising.

Frank gritted his teeth and gripped the rim of the basket with his chin and upper arms. Lifting his right leg, he slid his toes along the side of the basket. Somewhere there was a row of evenly spaced half-moon-shaped holes in the wicker for passengers to use as steps. If only he could find one and wedge his foot in it.

Suddenly, Svoboda let go of the burner lanyard and grabbed Frank's right arm with both hands. Desperate, Frank groped with his left hand and managed to hook it around Svoboda's knee. Taken by surprise, Svoboda jumped back and let go of Frank's arm.

At that moment, Frank's foot found one of the steps. He gathered his strength, ready to push himself up into the basket. But Svoboda had grabbed the fire extinguisher and was lifting it, ready to smash it down on Frank.

"Watch it, Svoboda," Frank gasped. "You've got crews from three TV networks and cable taping every move you make."

Svoboda blinked several times. He looked like someone who had just been shaken out of a daze. He dropped the fire extinguisher and stared down at Frank.

Frank took advantage and threw his leg over the rim, then pulled himself into the basket. Straightening up, he grabbed the red deflation cord and gave it a strong, steady tug. His stomach lurched as the balloon started to descend.

"No!" Svoboda shouted, trying to tear Frank's hand from the cord. "The prize! I'm going to lose the Lift Challenge!"

Frank pushed him hard. "Forget it, Svoboda," he said. "You lost a long time ago."

* * *

Svoboda's balloon landed in a pumpkin field just beyond the edge of the Wilderland property. As they touched down, several cars were already there, parked along the roadside. Joe and Chet were among the first to reach the basket. As Joe helped Frank climb out, he asked, "Are you okay?"

"I'm fine," Frank said. "Good thing I'm not scared of heights, though."

Fred Elwell came hurrying across the field, with Marie Thibault and Dave and Alicia Davidson close behind him. When Elwell came face to face with Svoboda, he barked, "You're a disgrace to the sport. I personally guarantee that once the police are through with you, you'll be barred from all IBC meets for the rest of your life."

Svoboda stared at him defiantly. Then, suddenly, his eyes fell.

"What did you do with the money?" Elwell demanded.

Svoboda stared up at him blankly. "Money?" he echoed. "What money?"

"The hundred thousand dollars you took from the office safe this morning," Elwell said. "Come on, admit it. You realized we weren't going to cave in to your demand, so you just stole the money."

"What are you talking about?" Svoboda

said. "I didn't steal any money. Maybe I broke a few rules, but I'm no petty criminal."

Frank tapped Elwell on the arm and whispered, "This could be a little complicated. He may not be the one. I'll explain back at the hotel."

As they all walked back to the waiting cars, Frank looked up at the ragged line of balloons, all heading east in pursuit of the big prize. Those that had already gained altitude were scarcely more than dots in the sky. Even so, Frank was sure he could make out the red, white, and green of *Windrider,* Paco Amaya's balloon, in the lead.

When the little convoy pulled up in front of the Wilderland, Max Arneson was waiting on the steps, practically bouncing from one foot to the other with anxiety. There were two state troopers waiting, too. One of them read Svoboda his rights, then they put him in the back of their car.

As the police car pulled away, Elwell asked Marie Thibault to set up the two-way radio on the veranda. Then he turned to Chet and the Hardys. "So let's hear it," he said. "How did you figure out it was Svoboda? And where's the money?"

"That's two separate questions," Joe replied. "As for the first one . . ." The three friends took turns explaining how they had finally narrowed their list of suspects down to Svoboda.

"So you're saying Mark Svoboda did the sabotage, but he didn't write the extortion notes?" Alicia said. "I don't get it. Was he working with somebody else?"

"Your dad was pretty convinced that fire yesterday morning at your balloon was an accident," Frank said. "We think he's right."

"But the second extortion note came right after the fire," Elwell said, "threatening more of the same."

"We know Svoboda was guilty of sabotage," Frank said, "and we're pretty sure he *wasn't* guilty of extortion."

"We think the extortionist committed one crime and one crime only," Chet said promptly. "Extortion."

"Right," Frank continued. "In other words, demanding money under menace. Writing those notes. Period. The extortionist never sabotaged anything. All he did was play along."

"I see," Alicia said. "After Mark Svoboda pulled that trick on Dutch Festinger, somebody else decided to take advantage of the situation by demanding the money."

"Exactly," Joe said.

"So who is it?" Arneson asked. "And where's the money?"

"We still don't know," Frank said. "What

we do know is it's somebody who had easy access to the computer."

"It's somebody who's comfortable on a motorcycle," Joe said, "and who wasn't seen around the hotel this morning between seven-thirty and nine. It's somebody who knew the money was in the safe and knew where to find the combination for the safe."

"And who had plenty of inside information on the meet," Chet added.

Elwell looked from Frank to Joe and back again. "Hold on a second," he said. "If I didn't know any better, I'd say you were talking about Marie Thibault. But that's impossible. Marie, tell them—" He looked around and realized she wasn't there anymore. "Where is she, anyway? I thought she went inside to get the radio. She should have been back by now."

Frank, Joe, and Chet all jumped to their feet and strode over to the front door of the hotel. Frank was already halfway inside when he heard the familiar racket of a motorcycle engine. He spun around and bumped into Joe.

"I'll get her!" Chet shouted. He ran down the steps and into the driveway, with Frank and Joe right behind him.

The purple motorcycle came shooting around the side of the building. The rider's helmet visor was up this time, and Frank could clearly see Marie Thibault's face showing her fear and panic.

"Chet, look out!" Alicia screamed. "Get out of the way!"

Chet, realizing he was about to be rammed by a thousand-pound motorcycle doing at least thirty-five miles an hour, reacted instinctively. He grabbed the nearest object, one of the orange rubber traffic cones that lined the drive. Raising it over his shoulder, he swung it straight at the onrushing rider's head.

Marie Thibault ducked but not in time. The traffic cone caught her a glancing blow on the side of her head, enough to knock her sideways. She lost her grip on the handlebars, and the front wheel left the pavement. The bike skidded sideways on the grass, and she jumped clear, somersaulting across the lawn. The bike fell on its side and slid another twenty yards, coming to a stop in a bed of rose bushes.

Joe was the first to reach her. He pulled off her knapsack and tossed it to Frank, then checked her for injuries. Frank handed the backpack to Elwell, who had come hurrying over from the porch.

"I'd be really surprised if you don't find the prize money in there," Frank said.

Thibault pushed Joe away and sat up.

"Why, Marie?" Elwell asked her. "Why

would you do something like this? After all the IBC has done for you?"

She scowled up at him. "Do you know what it feels like, tagging around for years after these people who go all over the world to balloon meets, when I can't even afford my own bike?" she demanded. "It was a shot at some real money, and I took it. It's just bad luck I didn't make it—bad luck and three teenage snoops."

Late that afternoon the group gathered again on the wide veranda of the Wilderland. The TV crews had packed up their equipment and driven off. The food concessionaires were busily dismantling their booths. As the last of the spectators headed for the parking area, the hotel's groundskeeping staff fanned out to pick up the mounds of litter.

The winner of the Lift Challenge—Paco Amaya—was dazzling in a bright red satin shirt embroidered with green vines and yellow flowers. He had changed into it for the award ceremony. As Frank, Joe, and Chet finished retelling how they had broken the case, Amaya shook his head in amazement.

"I almost feel sorry for Mark Svoboda," he said. "I had no idea he was so desperate to win. I thought *I* was the only one who wanted it that badly."

Max Arneson sat back in his chair, admiring the beautiful cloud-speckled sky. "Well, we're glad you won it," he said. "It's been an interesting weekend. And in spite of what I said before, I have to admit that ballooning and Lift soda are a pretty good sponsorship match. We've decided to stick with the Lift Challenge after all. Plus, we're going to become a major sponsor for Harris Scott's *Earthquest* project."

"We sort of guessed that's what all those mysterious meetings were about," Joe said.

Paco Amaya looked around the circle, then rested his gaze on Frank, Joe, and Chet. "I owe you guys one," he said. "Anytime you're in Albuquerque, look me up in the phone book—under Amaya Balloon Charters. It's not in there yet, but it will be as soon as I get home. I promise you a balloon ride that'll knock your socks off."

"That's great, Paco," Joe said. "But I'd like you to do one thing with your prize money before you sink it into your charter business."

"What's that?" Amaya asked.

Joe grinned and said, "Buy a really good chain lock for your motorcycle."

Frank and Joe's next case:

The Hardys are off to college, and they're about to get an education in deception, kidnapping, and murder. The boys already have an advanced degree in criminal investigations, so they've come to the right place. Frank and Joe are helping their friend Richie move into a dorm when Richie's roommate, Eli, is snatched by a couple of pistol-wielding thugs. Passions on campus are at a fever pitch. Eco-terrorists have vowed to stop construction of a chemical incinerator. Meanwhile, a visiting American diplomat, based in the war-torn country of Gabiz, had been targeted for assassination. Whoever is behind Eli's kidnapping is deadly serious—and the Hardys must take some serious action to bring him back alive . . . in *Clean Sweep,* Case #114 in The Hardy Boys Casefiles™.